About the Author

Morgan Dame was born in Las Vegas, Nevada, before moving to Kansas in high school, and then going to Missouri State University, where she got a degree in film and media studies. While at Missouri State, she took a short fiction class for an English credit. Long story short, after that class you are now holding this book.

Friendly Ghosts Make Good Company for Midnight Walks

Morgan Dame

Friendly Ghosts Make Good Company for Midnight Walks

Olympia Publishers
London

www.olympiapublishers.com
OLYMPIA PAPERBACK EDITION

Copyright © Morgan Dame 2023

The right of Morgan Dame to be identified as author of
this work has been asserted in accordance with sections 77 and 78 of
the Copyright, Designs and Patents Act 1988.

All Rights Reserved

No reproduction, copy or transmission of this publication
may be made without written permission.
No paragraph of this publication may be reproduced,
copied or transmitted save with the written permission of the publisher,
or in accordance with the provisions
of the Copyright Act 1956 (as amended).

Any person who commits any unauthorised act in relation to
this publication may be liable to criminal
prosecution and civil claims for damage.

A CIP catalogue record for this title is
available from the British Library.

ISBN: 978-1-80439-600-1

This is a work of fiction.
Names, characters, places and incidents originate from the writer's
imagination. Any resemblance to actual persons, living or dead, is
purely coincidental.

First Published in 2023

Olympia Publishers
Tallis House
2 Tallis Street
London
EC4Y 0AB

Printed in Great Britain

Dedication

To my mom, Kelsey, Garret, Maggie, and Shelby.

Acknowledgments

I would like to thank my mom for all her endless support and for doing homework with me as a kid. I remember and have heard I wasn't the nicest or the most grateful. I hope this book makes up for some of that. To Kelsey and Garrett, I imagine being my younger siblings isn't easy, but you both add so much color and happy experiences to my life. Although my dad is not alive to read this, it's worth putting in writing here that he taught me more than he'll ever know. More than a handful of great teachers and tutors come to mind that need thanking, actually, they deserve flowers every day for the rest of my life. I wasn't always a 'joy to have in class,' and even when I might have been, you all still deserve thanks for the support.

To my best friends Maggie and Shelby. I wanted to be friends with both of you before we were, so when I tell you both that I am just a fan and so impressed, I mean it. I can't wait to spend the rest of my life knowing you both.

Poking Through

I didn't need the movies, a song of heartbreak, or a passionate performance screamed atop the stage. My brother taught me everything I needed to know about spite and passion at the age of six. I'd like to think I have earlier memories. Sometimes, I look at photographs and I believe I remember flashes or instances of my earliest time. But really this was the first time my mind really decided to commit something to memory.

He was older, but not that old, still young enough that I don't think our parents thought he had it in him to do something so bold. I don't remember which one of my brother's offenses had earned it, but he had mere weeks left at our house before getting shipped off to boarding school.

I remember the day was hot, really hot, and he had just gotten back from the dentist. My parents must have thought that a few nitrous oxide hits and a half-paralyzed face was enough to trust leaving us home alone.

He had spread each of his limbs out dramatically on the recliner, a bag of frozen peas haphazardly laid across his face. At first, he seemed content sleeping off this minor life inconvenience.

Then he sprung up. In my memory, it was almost a dance or close to something you would see from an improv movement class. The grin that crowded my brother's half-paralyzed face was terrifying. He looked like an awful kid version of Harvey 'Two-Face' Dent. That inhuman relaxed frown next to a wide toothy smile.

"What?" I had asked, pulling at the straps of my overalls nervously.

"This is perfect," he answered me, but he was talking to himself. "Man, I couldn't have planned this better."

Then he was running, running to the other side of the house.

I half wanted to run in the other direction. Recently having learned my mom's full number, I should have called my mom at the grocery store and begged her to come home.

But I followed. Running at a good clip. I heard the drawers in the bathroom before I saw him.

Right now, our mom was getting soft foods for my brother to eat with his recently Novocain-inflicted mouth; and here he was, rummaging through her sewing kit which she left in the bathroom.

I remember asking him what he was doing, unlatching and latching my overalls, which I did as a kid; at one point, I forgot to latch the clasp again, leaving it dangling.

My brother answered without looking at me. He now had climbed into the sink, sitting applesauce-style in the bowl. He told me that his best friend Archie Brown had warned him it would hurt too bad if he did it himself.

He had a horrible, ugly, half-curled smile reflected in the mirror. He tapped his numb lip curiously, then manhandled it. Stretching it, daring it to feel anything.

I watched as he took his painted black-nailed fingers over the unopened needle kit.

Delicately, lovingly, peeling the plastic back. His breathing slowed, he pushed his long hair back, then he pulled out the size he wanted.

A long, skinny needle.

I backed up, but I couldn't blink.

Then with his eyes as wide as they would go and inches from the mirror, he pulled his lip forward and pushed the needle through the back. It sank through his flaccid Novocain-induced lip.

I never said another word to him. I couldn't. The more I watched the more my mouth hurt, the more I felt the texture of everything I wore. The edge of my ribbed socks on my ankles, the way the tag tickled my back, even the tightness of my new underwear. But my brother felt nothing.

It was nearly too much to watch. I understood why he wasn't in pain. But I didn't understand being an opportunist for a pierced lip. Why was he able to half-smile and enjoy the view of a needle sticking out of his dulled face?

His shoulders even relaxed, like he had finally been able to scratch an itch.

He was clumsy with the blood, like the lip was too fat or his fingers too wide. He smeared it too much. But he never lost his half-smile, his sense of focus.

My mom screamed and my dad had a dumbfounded, unable to comprehend face, but I don't remember the punishment. I think at the end of all of it, he was still going to be sent away. After all, what could they have done? Tell him not to do it again?

That's my first memory. The first time my brain logged something it wanted to know forever. It did more than just ruin the dentist for me. A school assigned D.A.R.E program full of methamphetamines and cocaine had nothing on my newfound fear of Novocain. Maybe my brain wanted to remember a life lesson, but that's far reaching; it just couldn't forget its first nightmare.

Hideouts and Freak-Outs

The lengthy dirt road felt much longer with my excitement bubbling over. I could barely read my comic; when I did look up from the page, it was just in time to see Kye fall.

"Kye!" I called down, hearing her tumble down to the ditch.

She had been "tightrope walking" on the lip of the road but had lost her balance.

Looking down, I could tell her knee was bleeding badly, and she was covered in twigs. However, she was more interested in brushing off grass from her *AC/DC* shirt. I had warned her not to try balancing like that to prevent something like this from happening. But the fact that I was twelve, and three years older than her, never seemed to hold very much water.

"I'm all right, Marty." She sounded almost bored.

"Byron should have Band-Aids at his house!" I knew she would be annoyed at my worry, but the blood on her knee had rolled down to her sock now.

"Like I care!" She clenched her jaw in embarrassment. She must not want Byron to know she had gotten hurt. And leaned down to brush off the blood with her hand.

I had to look away, blood always grossed me out. The sky was streaked with a nearly red horizon from the setting sun, leaving everything around us looking starkly orange and dark. Kye and I must have been walking for longer than I thought, and I didn't much like the idea of walking on our unlit dirt road at night. The nearby cottonwood and oak trees up the hill were nearly black, casting long winding shadows down the dying grass toward us. I sucked in their mixture of soft rustling leaves and sweet smell.

Normally, the effect was quite nice, but tonight it felt different. The orange clouds seemed closer together, and the trees seemed too dark. I was creeping myself out, but I couldn't shake the feeling that the trees were watching me.

Freaked, I pulled out Batman #509 from my backpack, I had packed every Dennis O'Neil comic I owned to show to Byron. His parents, for the first time in ages, were leaving him alone for a weekend. They were going on some couples' retreat; I hadn't the slightest idea what that was.

And I didn't think Byron really knew either, because all he knew (or cared about) was that they would be gone all weekend and drinking wine, while our mom was gone again on a marketing campaign to New York. So, we had all been struck with a bit of luck because this meant that this was the first time all three of us were parent-free for days.

"Hey, Marty." Kye had climbed back up to the road. "Mom left when I was taking Freddy on his walk, did I miss anything? Do you think she knows?"

I knew exactly what Kye was getting at. Although our mom had made a habit of leaving us alone, she wouldn't much like the idea of us spending a parent-free weekend at another house.

"No, she has no idea about Orson and Jessica being gone. She just said goodbye, you didn't miss anything." I let my hand harshly grip my comic. The truth was that she had just left a note for me when I had got out of the shower, mainly about how to take care of the house.

"Oh good!" Kye skipped ahead of me.

Byron's house wasn't too far off from ours, only a few miles.

Wallaceville was known for its vast farmlands. But our two families were a bit of an oddity for never farming. Although, back when my dad had been alive, he seemed to have wanted the land in the hopes of farming, but he wound up getting sick before he could. My mom admittedly only kept the property just because my dad had liked it. Byron and I had formed a friendship based on this in elementary school, given that the other kids just seemed to know our land to be wasted. So, we bonded over being mutually ignored. We enjoyed learning each other's differences; I taught Byron about comics, and he taught me tetherball at recess.

When we made it past the last thick row of cottonwoods, we reached Byron's beige house.

Byron had propped himself up on the house's deck, dangling his legs down. He was eating a green apple, and even from a distance I could make out that he had spiked up his blond hair with a healthy amount of gel. I almost laughed to myself wondering how long he had waited with his "cool" stance and apple ready. Kye, on the other hand, broke off into a run across the yellow grass towards him, her pink duffle bag bouncing behind her. Byron put the apple in his mouth and leaped down to hug her with both arms.

As I walked up, I smoothed my comic out. I had redrawn one of the pages to the best of my ability and wanted to show Byron how close I had gotten. As I got closer, I opened my mouth, but just then Byron got a funny grin on his face. He looked back between me and Kye, making sure he had our full attention.

"Are you guys ready to see some real horror movies?"

I dropped my comic. I knew Byron would have something like this planned but my stomach turned anyway.

"Oh! Mom would never let us see those!" Kye's eyes lit up

and began jumping up and down.

She wasn't wrong. My mom thought very poorly of scary movies and would have me and Kye be in our twenties before any would be in the house. Which I had liked just fine, but I knew it had been torture for Kye.

"A right shame if you ask me," Byron said with a broad grin toward Kye only.

Byron led Kye into the house. Left alone, I bent down to get my comic, brushing off the grass from Batman's face. Just then, I heard a loud crack behind me. I spun around. I was sure I had heard a twig snap, but what could have done it? Twigs didn't snap on their own. Freaked, I looked around. But all I could see was the dark woods and dying grass. Even though there was nothing to see, I couldn't shake the feeling of being watched by the trees.

"Marty, what's the hold up?" Byron called down, he had reappeared on his deck.

"Oh, nothing." I wasn't quite sure how to explain this one.

He laughed. "C'mon, I've got the house to show you!" His toothy grin helped me lose some of my fear.

Byron was absolutely ecstatic giving me and Kye a complete tour of his house. He walked through each room like a salesman giving us the "best of" every room. Though this time we were allowed into every room, the two rooms that we had previously not been allowed in were his parents' bedroom and his dad's study. I had always envisioned his dad's study. Most of my dad's things had been sold after his death, but I liked the idea of walking into a room full of his things.

Looking around the room seemed to warrant some of my swallowed jealousy. It was packed full of old movie posters, CDs, records, and sports paraphernalia. Mickey Rooney and The Godfather seemed to stare down at me. I let myself wonder briefly of what my dad would have had that Byron would have been jealous of. My eye caught a photo of Byron and his dad at a Red Sox game, both laughing with their same toothy grin.

"Your dad took you to a baseball game once, right?" Byron asked, catching my eye.

"Yeah, once." I paused. "I think it had been a Cubs game." This was a bit of a lie. I knew it was a Cubs game. It was one of the only photographs I had of me and my dad. And although we both looked happy in the photo, I had been too young to remember a thing.

"Hey, what's this?" Byron snatched the comic I was holding.

"Oh yeah!" I pulled my folder out of my bag and took out my pencil sketch of Batman.

The proportions were slightly off, but I was confident I had shaded it well.

Byron eyed the sketch with full admiration. "Man, I can't wait to see your art in a comic book. You should try to get into that fancy art school."

Amity High School was a private boarding school known for its art program. It was not only hard to get in to, but I would have to move two hours away.

"I don't know." I knew it would be great, but maybe in the way things were too good to be true. "But hey, you should try too." I knew Byron wanted to go too, not just because he wanted to get away from Wallaceville, but Amity also had a great sports program.

"C'mon, not with my grades, and anyway, you're the artist." He forced his broad smile.

"Not like he'll ever really be a comic book artist," interjected Kye, she had entered the room with one of Byron's trains. "You have to be able to stomach blood to draw it."

"Speaking of! Ready for *A Nightmare on Elm Street?*" Byron's eyes lit up something awful, Kye seemed to have woken him up to what was really important. All of his manic energy had re-emerged, but my face drained of color.

Just then, a loud but distant crash came from outside. I was the only one to jump, my head snapped towards the window. I was growing more worried, because once again I couldn't see anything to indicate what had made the sound.

Kye and Byron, on the other hand, didn't seem to share my worry. "Scared of a little thunder?" I could hear Byron's grin, and Kye's laughter.

He wasn't wrong. The orange clouds were beginning to take a dark shade of blue and it looked like it was going to rain. But it didn't sound anything like thunder. Inching closer, I squinted my eyes to the closest row of trees. The middle few trees' branches swayed slightly. But only the middle few trees, the rest of the trees sat still and unbothered. But for the middle trees' branches, it was as if something had just run through them. I swallowed hard and felt my unruly hair stick out straight on the back of my neck.

"Um, Marty? Care to come back?" Byron said with clear confusion.

"Yeah." I let myself have one last look before turning back to him. "Just thought I saw something." I tried to sound unfazed, and forced a particularly fake smile.

"The scaredy-cat's afraid of trees." Kye giggled, leaving the room. Byron chuckled and tailed behind her.

Now when I turned back toward the dark trees, I felt sick; being both alone and possibly watched. I wondered briefly how close of friends me and Byron truly were. In all honesty, I knew we didn't have very much in common. But maybe my worry was just anticipating that, sooner or later, he and Kye were going to be closer than I had ever been with him. Grabbing my bag, I wondered what I would do when that happened, and headed into the living room.

We all got into our pajamas and Byron made sure to turn off all the lights – in his already dark – living room off. Kye was gingerly getting the movie ready by rewinding the VHS with her eyes shut to avoid any spoilers. Byron was popping popcorn and by the smell of it, burning it. By the time we had all sat down and the movie started, it didn't take longer than the opening scene for me to realize what a terrible ride I was in for. I began to avert my eyes away from the screen. Never my head because I knew Kye or Byron would pick up on my head movement and call me out for being such a scaredy-cat.

I would focus my eyes on the popcorn ceiling, which now shone red and green from the movie. Or towards the window, it was now raining as predicted and the loud pitter-patter outside made the horror-filled living room feel, if nothing else, safer than the outside world. I forced what I could out of my head and tried to keep my mind occupied with anything other than the movie.

Things like, Kye chewing loudly, wood boards outside creaking. At one point, I looked at Byron, who was reclined completely back on his dad's La-Z-Boy recliner, shoveling his charred popcorn into his mouth. He looked quite humorous, the chair was clearly meant for someone much taller than him, he was reclined so far back that it was clear he never got this seat typically. But more so than anything, I got the feeling that he was trying to look cool.

Looking back over, the main girl Nancy was in the bathtub falling asleep, I couldn't see that ending well so my eyes went back to the window. The rain and slight yellow reflection of the living room was all I could make out, but it was better than being scared. I imagined getting through horror movies like this gave people like Byron a sense of bravery. Unlike me, who was just getting my cowardice further proven.

But then the window changed.

So odd. I suddenly couldn't make out anything. No rain, no reflection, the window was suddenly solid black. Weird. What could have taken the light from the window? Only something right in front of it? *Don't think about that, you're just being scared, playing tricks on yourself, sensing movement that's not there.* But what about the trees and twigs from earlier? Now the black outside the window felt like it was moving. My curly hair had been stuck to the back of my neck before, but now goosebumps pricked through.

Then a snow-white hand pressed itself against the glass.

"Kye, Byron! Look!" I barely managed a whisper, but I knew I was louder than the movie.

Kye was curled up against the couch, knees in her chest, starry-eyed at the screen. She tore her eyes away and looked at me with a mixture of annoyance and confusion.

"I know, right, this scene always gets me too." Byron had not looked at me but had stayed in his reclined stance, watching the knife-tipped fingers go back into the tub.

"Not the movie!" I said annoyed. "The window…" But now the hand was gone. The window shined once again with rain and only reflected my own scared face back at me.

Kye and Byron were sharing a look to each other when I turned back. To them, I seemed to have called wolf too many times in one night.

"There was a hand," my voice pleaded, but I knew whatever I was about to say was going to fall flat. Kye and Byron couldn't look less worried if they wanted to. Kye was waiting for me to be done, she still had her hand on the remote ready to press play.

Byron looked skeptical. "Did the hand look like the one in the movie, like it was reflected on the glass?"

"No, dude... it didn't even have the glove." I was sure Byron thought I had lost it.

I turned back to the window, I swallowed my dry mouth and peered out into the darkness. I really didn't want to see anything, but I also wanted some form of proof. But the rain and night sky didn't let me see past the porch.

"Can't we just make sure all the doors are locked?" I tried to make my voice sound reasonable or sane, like this was in everyone's best interest.

"Ugh, I'm going to go get popcorn," Kye said, removing herself.

Byron looked at her with understanding before turning back to me, "Sure, sure. We'll lock doors. So long as you quit your crying." He got up slowly, removing his blanket like it was a chore.

I had expected something like this to be said. But in the moment, I was too worried to care, I was beginning to feel like I was in a fishbowl. Every hallway in his small house was only lit by the paused TV screen, the effect made the whole situation worse.

"Do you really think I'm making this up?" I asked Byron, even if he didn't believe it himself, I needed something.

He paused. "No." He looked at me in a regretful sort of way. "You really think you saw something."

We locked the front door and all the windows in the living room before heading to the back door in the kitchen. Kye was still there, but instead of getting popcorn she was standing in front of the screen door, peering out. The light from the very distant TV was ghoul-lighting her. Crisp yellow light on her back against the nearly black, giant rainy doors. She looked so eerie. Then she looked over her shoulder at us, wide eyed and crying.

"Marty was right." She could barely get the words out. "Someone's walking around the house."

My heart sank from her validation. I was now petrified, the room felt twenty degrees colder. Looking at Kye, I could see all of the fear she would normally try, and succeed, to hide. But now she was holding herself together with her little arms; she looked sickly. Something broke inside me, seeing her so horrified. For the first time in a while, I saw the nine-year-old girl under her strong demeanor. I went over and hugged her.

"OK, but let's talk about this. I mean, Christ…" I turned over to Byron, stumbling over his words. "Are we really suggesting someone is watching the house?" His mouth hung half open and eyes looked terrified, nothing like the kid with spiky hair and apple.

"Byron, c'mon." I motioned my head to Kye, he knew this wasn't normal for her.

His eyes contracted, trying to find something that could prove this wasn't what it was. The phone rang.

We all stopped. Looked at the phone. Then back to each other. Then back to the phone. Kye was holding her breath as tears streamed down her face. Byron looked frozen in time. His blond hair and light skin both looked paper white. He walked over like a ghost, like his feet had no real want to take him anywhere. I trailed behind him.

He cleared his throat and picked up the landline. "Hi?" His eyes welled up. Nothing but rain and breathing could be heard.

He inhaled sharply, tears streaming down his face as he

slammed the phone down.

Almost like he was a mixture of offended and terrified.

"Oh, God... Are we going to die?" Kye's eyes looked haunted.

"Go to the couch and stay there. Tell us if you hear anything." I walked over and gripped her hand. "And no." Her thinking that alone wasn't something I could handle.

Byron and I began tearing his house apart, looking for anything that had a snowball's chance of helping us. The slow movement of before was of a time gone by. Now every window and door were definitely locked. Byron had found his dad's switchblade and we agreed that it was the best bet of defending ourselves. We also had found a flashlight and had given it to Kye, but we wished we hadn't. She was on the couch looking like she was in a trance, seeing something not there, gripping her small flashlight so tightly in her hands they were paper-white, shining the light at the door expecting the figure to walk right in.

Admittedly, we had made a mess of the kitchen tearing it apart, laying out everything that had a chance of helping us. Standing on the kitchen table, we surveyed the pathetically small pile. Mostly toy weapons that at least were sharp, a few kitchen knives, and a baseball bat. All that was left was to call the cops. We seemed to have saved this part for last. Actually, telling the adults seemed to make it real, proof that what we had seen was more real than smoke and mirrors and movies.

I picked up Byron's home phone, we both stared at it. It felt heavy in my bony hand. I looked up at his face, he was still looking at the phone. His previously spiked up blond hair was flopping over his eyes, all the coolness he tried to prove seemed drained out of him. Staring at the phone like it was now something of a nightmare.

Even with all my cowardly bones, I thought, *You can't make him do it.* "I'll call."

"Really, Marty?" His voice cracked. I had expected him to sound shocked, but he sounded grateful.

Well, here goes nothing. I sucked in some air and dialed. The operator that answered sounded like a young woman. I told her everything I could about our situation. My fear was proven, listing off everything stacked against us made the situation both more real and more terrifying. In all reality, we were one nine and two twelve-year-olds in a house in the middle of the woods with no adults, far out from a city, with a strange figure walking around the house. I thought back to the trees, snapping twigs, crashing, and phone calls. I couldn't shake the discomfort that this figure had probably been watching us for hours.

I waited for her, hoping she could say something, anything, that could make this better, that somehow my anxiety and panic had made things worse than they really were. However, when she spoke, she seemed like she was masking her discomfort by sounding overly nice. The reality was, the police station was deep in town, and we were far away. So, it would be over half an hour until they could get to us. But she sweetly reassured me that she would stay on the line with me the whole time. The situation didn't feel quite saved but the promise to be saved had a nice effect. I felt my shoulders loosen up and I turned back to Byron, who was now standing next to Kye on the couch, holding hands.

As quickly as hope had come, it left. Because then it went from bad to worse.

A big crash suddenly broke the silence. It sounded the way I thought gunshots or car accidents must sound. What's more, it sounded like it had come from the inside of the house. From Byron's dad's study.

I dropped the receiver and ran to Kye and Byron who had frozen from fear. I grabbed Kye's arm. Byron unfroze and ran to the door. I took Kye and followed him. He fumbled with the lock just long enough for me to think it was all over. The door opened, releasing us to a soaked deck. I took a moment to shut the door behind us, just barely hearing the last bits of comfort from the receiver. Then all I could hear was the rain, violent trees, and howling wind.

Kye was grabbing at my hand, and we slogged through the mud to Byron. It was like running in a nightmare, it was slow difficult work and it felt like the figure was right behind us. The rain was a rude awakening, it was cold, not just for the summer, but too cold. Kye was in her pajama shorts and a *Star Wars* T-shirt. Byron wasn't even wearing a shirt and only had his plaid pajama pants on. And I was in my high-water pair of pajama pants and a black T-shirt. And we were all barefoot.

By the time Kye and I met Byron at the wood's edge, we were covered in mud up to our knees. All of my clothes were soaked, and rain dripped from my hair streaming down my face like fat tears. Once we managed to get inside the trees, it blocked some of the rain, but the drops that did hit were huge and felt even more like ice than the ones before. Everything was black and hard to see, in a moment of wishful thinking I wanted nothing more than to be anyone else in the world.

I couldn't think of a time when I was more uncomfortable. I turned around and tried to hear for anyone following us, but all I could make out was the mud, hard rain, howling wind, and the leaves and twigs snapping at our feet. Then my foot hit a slick patch of mud and I slipped, falling hard.

Pain flashed over my eyes. I could feel twigs lodge into my leg. I knew it was bleeding before I jumped back up, the sudden ache woke me up to something awful. Kye and Byron both turned around. I ran to them but it wasn't the same as before. My foot was rigid, and the ground felt like it was pushing itself into my leg all the way up to my knee. Now the only thing that felt somewhat warm was the blood running down my leg. I couldn't make out their faces, but they knew things had changed, we couldn't keep running.

I felt awful, like I pushed them into the mud with me.

"Let's find a place to hide," Byron whispered in my direction. His words were final... But I caught a glance in his eyes and they showcased his fear.

We lay down on a decent pile of leaves by a wide cottonwood. We each found a portion to lay flat on, and as quietly as we could manage, cover ourselves in leaves. And then it was quiet. We all began to focus on staying still. But the sudden stillness let the cold set in. The running at least had taken our minds off it enough, but now Byron was shivering violently, and I could hear Kye was having a hard time with her teeth knocking together. She shifted to force her mouth closed. My leg was throbbing, but it was also now the only limb I could feel. Every part of me began to feel like numb hunks of meat.

My mind went to the mysterious figure who may or may not be on their way to find us. Even though we called the cops, and they were on their way to the house, the police had no idea where we were in the woods, or that we went to the woods. Even if this was a good hiding place from the figure, it also kept us hidden from the cops. Every fear I'd ever had felt small and inadequate to this moment. Although it was my life's most warranted moment to be scared, I'd never felt more like a coward.

After a few minutes, I was hyper aware of a drop of water coming from the tree that continued to hit my back. It froze my spine the first few times, then it carved into it. Painfully stinging it and reminding me of how painful my feet and hands had become. My nostrils burned from sucking in the cold air. Every winter of my life couldn't have prepared me for what true coldness is. It's a brutal constant. It felt like the sort of cold that kills people. I closed my eyes and tried to think of anything warm. Egypt, deserts, fire, hot coco, a jacket, a blanket. To be in bed, to feel my hands again.

To be brave.

The way Batman runs towards danger, to fight, to protect. For a moment, I thought about getting up from my scared hiding place and going toward the bad guy. Standing there, my leg bleeding, prepared to die. The way Batman does for Gotham, the way parents die for their kids. The way I had promised Kye we weren't going to die.

"Marty?" It was Kye, she was whispering. "It's so cold." Her voice sounded thick.

I opened my eyes, Kye had crawled her way into my arms. Her head laid down close to my chest. I tried to pull her in tighter, but everything's wet and my hands felt too numb, unable to do basic tasks. I quit trying, hoping somehow, I was making her warmer. I called out to Byron to come closer, but I didn't hear him.

I was so tired, I shut my eyes.

My sense of time was long gone, but the cold made it feel like forever. I could barely feel Kye anymore. This felt like an end. I wished I could have done more for Byron and Kye, fought the fear from their eyes. I know people die, my dad did, but I had told Kye it wasn't going to happen.

Movement worked its way into my head. *Stay still,* I didn't want the figure to find us. I heard sounds but I couldn't make out what they were. It was too cold. The world seemed both still and brutally happening. I worked to open my eyes; lights clouded my vision. In a weird way, I didn't think it was real. I shut my eyes. But the movement felt closer now. Closing in. This was it. The figure had found us. We were going to die.

Focus. I'm being lifted off the ground. GO. RUN. My limbs failed me, and I couldn't go, they moved without direction and without clear signals. They were floppy and uncoordinated, and I really was just a cold child.

I opened my eyes. The light blinded me again, but not for long. I adjusted slowly to my surroundings, the trees backlighted the dark sky, and my hair plastered my wet face. I focused straight on the light burning my eyelids something awful. It was a white orb, just like a flashlight. It was being held by a worried-looking man, he was holding me and had a badge, he slipped his wet rain jacket over me.

"Calm down, son. Calm down, it's gonna be all right."

It's actually real? It's actually real. Fear drained out of me so quickly I wondered if I'd pass out from relief. The man held me in a sort of parental way, cradling all my weight in his arms. My burning eyes looked over, another cop was holding Kye, pressing her up to his shoulder, and she was completely encased in the cop's giant raincoat. I whipped my head awkwardly over to Byron's direction; the lady cop's jacket had been wrapped around him tightly like a sleeping bag and I can tell his ragged breathing had calmed down considerably.

The cop was still telling me not to worry and that they were going to be all right. I exhaled all the cold air from my lungs and let the man fully support my weight. Hoping to never have a night like this one again.

Should I Measure My Fears in Nights or Years?

I shot my phaser in the direction the hissing sound had come from. The red and purple flashes only illuminated a particularly dirty corner from under my bed. I exhaled; I was hanging upside down on my bed, only now completely in the shadows. The moon and my alarm clock were the only lights, ten forty-seven p.m.

I rolled onto my back to stare at the ceiling, placing my phaser on my stomach. The sound I had heard was unlike anything I could rationalize, almost a snake-like hissing. Although relieved to not find anything, I disliked that I had no leads as to what the sound could have possibly been, or where it had gone to.

A sudden creaking sound broke my concentration. I flipped over and pointed my phaser at my door; the sound was now coming from outside my bedroom. I got up and tiptoed to my door, keeping my phaser in hand, though I was well aware that the toy was in no position to do anything more than light up.

I heard some creaking; the thing was definitely outside my door. I shut my eyes, exhaled, flicked my eyes open. Then I opened my door, pointed my phaser and fired in one swift motion.

The flashing lights illuminated his reaction in distinct phases, like a strobe light making real time look slow motion.

My brother's eyes widened with shock and fear. He dropped his car keys, and they landed in a heap on the carpet. Then he registered the purple and red lights. His eyebrows moved down to an annoyance, but a sort of relief went over him. He collapsed his weight against the wall with an exhaustion that seemed older than him. The purple and red lights really highlighted the rounded bags under his eyes.

A mixture of guilt and embarrassment came over me. I should have realized it was Dennis. Although I wasn't allowed to know why, my sixteen-year-old brother had been in the worst trouble of his life the past six months. I had put together that it was something to do with his best friend Hiroki. He now was forbidden to see Hiroki, or see any of his baseball friends for that matter. I was hard pressed to think of what my brother did to deserve this kind of punishment. He always had an annoying respect for the rules.

"I'm sorry if I scared you, Dean," Dennis whispered, crouching down to my level.

"Where were you?" I whispered a little loudly, my curiosity overtaking me.

Dennis shut his eyes, short enough to be a blink, but too long for me to fully believe that. "Were you with Hiroki?"

He paused. "Yes."

I nodded.

"You won't tell on me?"

I shook my head. I wasn't sure what my brother had done, but never seeing a friend again had earned my sympathy.

"Good." He regained his height. He glanced at my left hand and smiled a little sadly. "Were you going to shoot me, Captain Kirk?" he whispered.

I smiled. "I did shoot you," I corrected. Looking at the carpet and feeling a little bashful. "I heard a weird noise, so I wanted to find it." I dug my foot into the carpet, looking down. My brother was seven years older than me, but always made a point to let me explain myself.

He laughed, then covered his mouth. He gripped my shoulder tightly, looked me in the eyes. "Fear not, there are no monsters, it was just me."

I felt childish and went back to my room. Dennis had the wrong idea – I hadn't intended to find a real monster, but an answer to the sound. I wasn't in my shadowed room long before I noticed something wrong.

My room seemed to lack its previous color. I rubbed my eyes, expecting to adjust to the dark room, but it stayed the same; it looked like it was on our black and white TV.

Before I could think to turn on the lights, a weird feverish sensation came over me. My hair flew behind me. My body chilled as my head became hot and dizzy. Almost a draining sensation came over me. I struggled to stand. Clammy, cold sweat was forming on my palms.

I gripped my phaser tightly and shot, though there were now black and white flashes emitting from my toy. I gasped, then my eyes fixated on the only color I could see, a pair of deep yellow eyes under my bed. If I could have seen its mouth, it would have been smiling.

Then the floor slid open like a matchbox. I reached up, stupidly grasping at air before I fell. My body was falling faster than I could register; opening my eyes, all I could make out was my striped pajamas thrashing violently against my limbs. The only reason I knew this wasn't a dream when I landed was because I still had my phaser.

To my surprise I hadn't landed in pain, but more like I had come up from the ground.

I was lying in an inch of water. The water was so shallow it was annoying. It drenched the back of my curly hair and the back half of my body. It seemed to eerily match my body temperature, like staying in the bathtub to enjoy the last bits of warm water.

I scanned my eyes around and took in my surroundings. I was in a room of mirrors; dozens and dozens of me were looking around, repeated countless times. The room itself was really about the size of a classroom. Looking up, I noticed that the ceiling mirror shined both a bird's-eye view of me, and oddly, the night sky.

There were two other kids with me, who looked like they were either in my grade or the next.

The girl seemed more composed and curious. She had straight, deep brown hair that was down to her waist, and dark curious eyes. She was wearing plaid pajamas and a shirt that said *Rear Window*.

The boy had a drenched, stuffed toy cat that he was clutching protectively. He was in matching, what looked like, silk pajamas. He couldn't have been standing more vertical, which might have come across brave or powerful, if he didn't look so drained.

"Where am I?" I wanted to say something braver or smarter.

The girl shook her head. "Wait," she whispered, pressing her index finger to her lips.

Then the mirrors seemed to darken in shades, fading what I could see. The gold eyes caught mine and seemed to smile once more, repeated over and over again in all the mirror images. The water seemed colder now, and smoke flooded the room like a fog.

"You're here and well, leave, and this is what you will become."

My head snapped back painfully, and images took over my eyelids. Years and time stretched my body dramatically into a longer, fuller form. I was now older than Dennis, but I seemed off. I felt almost deranged. I had aged skin and a soreness to my body, but I was still too young to feel like this.

I was on a cold mountainside. The clouds began to part in the night sky by Orion's belt.

My teeth ripped into my lips and parts of me were growing and some shrinking. My fingernails grew rapidly and thick, carving into and out of my fingertips painfully. The world melted into black and white. Then snapping twigs worked their way into my feverish mind.

Turning, I saw Dennis scared and horrified, this time no relief meeting his eyes. "Stay back!" I yelled before my animalistic mind completely took over.

It took me a moment to realize I was back with my normal body; it seemed outrageously small. I was now lying curled up, face down in the inch-deep water. I was covered in a sheen of cold sweat and breathing heavily. I had both my hands and phaser clutched to my chest. I couldn't tell if my face was only wet from the water, so I wiped it regardless.

The girl's hand was on my shoulder. I sniffed once and tried to regain some composure. "What did the ghost show you?" she whispered.

I took a moment. "Ghost?"

"We just call it that," she clarified. "I'm Edith. That's Wallace." She nodded to the stiff boy.

"Dean," I mumbled. I looked them both over for a moment.

They both seemed scared and lost in their own way. Edith, though more calm in composure, still had big wide eyes that scanned the room constantly. I glanced over at the boy, Wallace. What fear Edith had in her eyes was written all over him. He seemed out of sorts in an almost shell-like way; his skin had a dull waxiness to it, like he couldn't muster color in a state of such fear. I turned back to Edith, remembering her question.

"I'm not sure what I saw, I..." I tried thinking it over, but I was having trouble focusing on one thing.

"Guess."

"I think," I took a moment to come to terms with the ridiculousness of what I was going to say. "I think I was a werewolf."

"Really?" Edith sounded almost impressed.

"Yeah." I felt around my fingertips, relieved at their normalcy. "But seriously, what's going on? I was just going to bed when..."

"When you fell through." Edith guessed correctly. "The same happened to me and Wallace. Wallace was first, it seems we each got taken and—"

"And now we can't go back without a curse." This time, it was Wallace who had spoken. His voice lacked any sort of power. If this boy had any bravery in him, I couldn't see or hear it.

"Yes." Edith's eyes flashed for a moment at Wallace in maybe an annoyed agreement. Though not impervious to fear, she seemed almost lost in thought before she continued. "If Wallace goes back, everything he touches will become stone." My eyes moved to Wallace who seemed to hold his soaking cat even harder. I took a moment to entertain the idea of a curse like that.

"And you?" Almost instantly, I wished I hadn't asked. Edith's face fell, her jaw shifted before she spoke.

"I would be sent back invisible. I would call out to my parents, but they would never see me." She said it with almost a coldness, though it was clearly just to hide her emotions.

"Is there anything else you know?" I didn't know how to even begin to solve a problem like this.

Edith thought this over. "Well, I have a few guesses. The ghost isn't always here, like I don't think it's here now." She paused to scan around once more. "There also seems to be a new kid every two days." She looked up at the night sky in the mirror. "At least I think two days."

I turned to look around the mirror room. It was almost dizzying trying to inspect a room that was duplicated over and over in every direction. There seemed to be no objects or anything. Not even a door. I wanted to be back home in my bed so deeply; it was nightmarish how out of sorts and lost I felt.

"What's that?" Wallace asked.

I turned to Wallace, whose fantastic posture still took some getting used to. "What?"

"The toy… gun?" Even though he was clearly ruled by fear, he seemed taken by my phaser.

I reached my hand up to my wet head awkwardly. I knew enough that *Star Trek* wasn't popular with everyone at my school, so I mostly kept it to myself. But this hardly seemed the time to get bashful. "It's a phaser." I paused before admitting, "From *Star Trek*."

"Trek?" He looked thoughtful. "I've never heard of it."

"Oh, It's a TV show, Thursdays, at eight thirty, NBC." I would have stopped at TV show, but Wallace seemed to have no idea what I was talking about.

He took a moment. "No, that cuts into *Hour Glass*," he corrected.

I aimed my eyebrows down. Maybe Wallace was just as pompous as he was fearful. "Anyway," Wallace continued, "my nanny lets me watch anything, and I've never heard of this Trek."

He seemed the type, I thought dully. Though it was odd. "Well, I've never seen *Hour Glass*," I said defensively.

"You should." He was stroking his dripping cat. "They sing, and dance, not quite *Meet Me in St. Louis*, but still really good.

Are you allowed to watch TV when you want?" He had his chest puffed out obnoxiously.

I shifted my eyebrows down. "Well, I can't watch much TV. My mom thinks they'll talk about the war, or Russia. Though they never do."

Wallace had grown on my nerves, which was impressive considering the circumstances. I turned to Edith. To my surprise, she seemed deeply confused.

"Why would they still be talking about the war?" Wallace asked.

"Edith?" I ignored Wallace.

She was standing very still, almost Wallace's posture. Her face seemed ghastly.

"What war are you talking about?" Edith looked up with almost regret.

How odd. My eyebrows turned down. Surely even my most shielded friends knew about the Vietnam War. But both Wallace and Edith were looking at me oddly.

"Well." I paused. "You know, the Vietnam War."

Wallace pompously sniggered, but Edith's already wide eyes turned up even higher.

Edith took a moment; she seemed to be deciding on her words before asking, "What year is it?"

What was she driving at? Didn't we have bigger problems? "1968." I said this with almost a pompousness myself; surely this much was obvious.

However, Wallace's pompous face took on a confusion. When I shifted my eyes back to Edith and saw her face, I realized, as she had. Edith sank to her knees in the water, the tips of her long hair getting wet (though she didn't seem to notice).

"And for you?" I regretted the question as much as I would

37

hate the answer.

"It is." She stopped. "It was 1957."

My head went slack on my shoulders.

Wallace's reaction came in phases. First, he looked at us both with exasperation, almost hoping we were both insane. Before he put together that we, unfortunately, were telling our own truths.

"You're lying." He wasn't accusing me or Edith, more the world. He turned like a wind-up toy back and forth between us. He looked quite idiotic with his floppy, blond hair swishing to and fro. It would have been humorous if I felt like laughing. "Please," he begged. "This isn't true."

Edith unfroze herself and put one hand on Wallace's shoulder. She opened her mouth to say something but thought better of it.

After a while (perhaps ten minutes, though probably longer), Wallace told us that it was the year 1946 to him.

This realization of years passing each of us by had caused a quietness. We sat by one another in a triangle shape. Though I wanted to believe that no time had passed, it could easily be 1970 (or later) by the time I found a way out, if it wasn't already. I wondered what I had missed. Childishly, I looked down at my toy phaser. Bitterly – or even stupidly – thinking of the weeks of *Star Trek* I had missed.

I also thought of Wallace and Edith though. So, the war that Wallace had mentioned was World War II. To him, it had just finished. And he also hadn't been wrong to say *Hour Glass* was on at eight thirty, because it must have been true. I looked at Edith's *Rear Window* shirt, which would have come out recently for her. I looked at the two of them with a more mystical nature. Despite their looks, both of them were technically older than Dennis.

So even if we found a way out, what would we find?

I then thought for a moment about the curse I had been given. I wondered if I were to go back, would I actually be a werewolf? I looked past my phaser, at my hands, allowing myself to fully consider the horror. I had never considered the idea of really becoming something else. Dennis had been right, there were no such things as monsters. But that would change if I went home.

Could I manage that life? Keep it a secret? I thought sadly, how could I still look up at Captain Kirk and see myself?

Then I considered Wallace touching only stone, a prison slowly of his own making. Or Edith's habitual loneliness, forever having to convince the world she was real and existed.

But then I looked past my hands at my scared reflection.

What if I locked myself up on full moons, or Wallace covered his hands, or Edith poured water or paint on herself? Yes, all curses remained. But we were forewarned, were we not? I thought of my cold mountainside scene, yelling at Dennis to stay back. Could my knowledge of the future be enough to change it?

Although everything was telling me to stay, I knew I would have to try and escape. Then I really looked down.

Odd. If the water was so shallow, why could I not see the ground? All I could make out was what everything else looked like. A reflection. I pressed my hands into the ground. To my surprise, the ground I could not see seemed unsolid enough. Like clay that had hardened but, with enough force, could change its shape once more.

I began to try and move the shallow water away from the ground, to see something other than my own reflection. Just what did this ground look like? As soon as I pushed some water away, it was refilled. I continued and continued. My pushing away became a splashing, which became more and more mad. I seemed to be letting all my frustrations out versus expecting any real escape. I grabbed my phaser and began hitting the ground, just to change it, to make some dent, dig a way out. Then, to my surprise, I felt the ground going deeper. I was escaping. It was working.

I didn't notice the smoke roll in.

It was Wallace's screaming that made me stop dead in my tracks and turn.

His arms had fallen off. His cat lay between the two arms. The limbs seemed to have fallen out of their sleeves. They looked the way a Barbie doll's arms would if they popped off. It was almost worse to see no blood, just two hunks of arms lying like objects on the floor.

Edith had run over to Wallace. What I was seeing seemed so far away from me. I couldn't have said if Edith was screaming too or even what Wallace really looked like.

"Quit trying to escape."

The voice spoke almost in a scolding manner, but slowly and deliberately. The moment the voice finished, the room snapped back to form so quickly that I had to blink to adjust to it.

Wallace's arms were back on his body, and he was gripping his cat so tightly that the water it had soaked up was spilling back onto the ground. I turned back to the hole I had started to make; it had refilled.

So, if I were to try and leave of my own accord, I wouldn't be the one punished. We were forced to all agree on leaving or staying. If I made the choice to touch fire, why wasn't I the one getting burned?

It took some time to calm Wallace down. Once his breathing slowed back to normal, I wondered how to begin to apologize.

"So, is this it?" Wallace wondered softly, opening his eyes and clearing the fur away from the stuffed cat's eyes so it could see clearly too.

"Wallace," Edith said tentatively. Looking at her, I was surprised by her expression. I felt as though this was a new low but she seemed lost in thought.

He sniffed. "Yes?"

"Can I ask you a question?"

He nodded stiffly.

"Don't get mad, but..." She paused, mulling something over. "Did it hurt?" What an odd question. Of all the things, this seemed to be missing the point.

Wallace blinked a few times, his wet face dumbstruck. Almost like he was really looking at her for the first time, and not liking what he saw. But then his expression changed.

"No. No, it didn't hurt," he admitted.

"That's what I thought." She was now looking past him.

"What are you thinking?" I asked before stopping myself.

"Well." A bashful look came over Edith. "Really don't get mad, Wallace," she warned with sympathy. "It really looked like your arms fell off."

"They did!" Me and Wallace both said. Our eyes met and we half smiled at our overlapping agreement.

"I know," she said, more annoyed. "But I've been thinking." She paused. She looked around the room with almost an unimpressed look. "When Wallace's arms fell off, why did the ghost take the time to cover the room in smoke? It didn't need to." She thought for a moment. "Why was there no blood? It's like they didn't fall off at all."

"What, do you think it didn't happen?" I asked.

"My arms really fell off," Wallace said with a sad pompousness I expected from him, but I also agreed with him.

"I'm saying that maybe the ghost can make it look like your

arms fell off, without having to really remove them," Edith clarified.

I thought about this. Maybe it was like the age-old trick of "taking someone's nose" or the quarter behind the ear. I had looked at the arms on the floor but didn't think to look at Wallace to check if they had really fallen. Was I so stage managed, seeing what it wanted me to? I looked around; none of this could exist. Was it all really some messed up funhouse, a house of mirrors?

"You're right, Edith." I looked up at her. "But not all of it. Some of this is real, we're really here, and we're all really from different times."

"I agree," she whispered. "The ghost took us here, but it's convincing us to stay."

"But wait!" Wallace held up his hand. "Okay but, so what? I mean, if we go back, we're cursed, right?"

It was a fair point. Even if some of it wasn't real, the problem remained; it would still be a gamble to try and leave.

"Maybe not." Edith pondered this. "Each curse is something we could have thought of ourselves, right? Maybe based on our own fears." She looked around at us. "Werewolves? Invisibility? and…" She paused. "Is it Medusa or King Midas that scared you?" Edith asked Wallace.

"Both," he admitted with a small smile.

So maybe it wasn't infallible. "Okay, let's hatch a plan," I said. My chest felt like it had air for the first time since being here.

We whispered about ways, ideas, and things we could do to escape. All ideas came with their own problems and their own questions. We had also decided to stop calling it The Ghost but instead The Magician. It didn't change anything really, but it had an honest sense of rebellion to it. We couldn't stop ourselves, even Wallace, from smiling slyly whenever we called it that. We decided eventually on a sub-par plan, but with the hope that it would be enough.

But we were tired.

I had never tried to sleep in water before. I was now fully soaked and had grown cold. I kept my phaser at my chest though I knew it was false protection. I looked up at myself in the night sky, right next to the Big Dipper. I sighed. This place did have a regretful sort of beauty to it. I looked over at Edith; our eyes met in the mirror.

"Dean?"

"Yes?"

She paused. "So... so, there's going to be another war?"

I paused. "Yes."

She sighed; her eyes shifted away from mine.

I thought for a moment about how I would feel in her shoes, learning the future, and it losing its excitement.

"It's not so bad," I said, though I knew this was a dumb thing to say.

She laughed quietly. But did seem to consider it. "Even if I do get sent back to my time" – she sighed – "I'll have to keep that secret."

I wondered. "Maybe you shouldn't." I looked around the stars. "Maybe you, or Wallace, can change it." Our eyes shifted to the reflection of Wallace, using the wet cat as a pillow, who even in his sleep had a posture that was remarkable. Like a mummy frozen in place.

"No."

I sat up to really see her. "Why not?" My eyebrows turned down. "You guys could save so many people." I felt a weird sort of jealousy. I envied their position.

"No, Dean. If I or Wallace tried, or did that," she stopped to pick her words, "we could make things worse, or change your life."

"Fine." I laid back down. It was a fair point, even an obvious one. Maybe it was more of a curse. Knowing things that no one else can know yet. Scared to do anything you weren't supposed to. But it could be a worthy gamble to try to change it for the better.

"I still think it could be worth changing," I said.

Edith seemed to be sizing me up. "This is bigger than you, Dean."

Edith sounded almost condescending. Sure, she had a point, but didn't I as well? If we knew it was going to be bad anyway, wasn't that worth changing my life and others'?

"Why do you think The Magician took us?" Edith asked, breaking my thoughts. I pondered this.

"Do you think it needs us for something?"

"I thought that at first," she said.

"But not anymore?"

"Well, this seems an awful lot like a fishbowl," she said.

"Would you put so much time into collecting a few fish?" I asked.

"I think so." She paused. "I know when my dog tries to leave, I try to get him back."

It was an annoying thought. That I was taken for such a trivial purpose. But The Magician hadn't done anything with us. Just watched and told us to stay. Was I really just a decoration on a wall?

"Dean?"

"Yes?"

"Thanks for volunteering."

It wasn't changing the world, I thought bitterly. "Think nothing of it."

Edith turned on her side, exhaled a little sadly and said, "Goodnight, Dean." Her long, wet hair draped down her side.

"Goodnight, Edith."

Wallace was the one shaking my shoulder to get me up the next morning. I put my hand to my eyes, forgetting my hand was wet.

"Dean? Dean?" He sighed. "C'mon, I want to ask you something."

I stopped myself from asking what time it was. It didn't matter how many hours – or really years – I had slept, I thought sourly. "What?"

"Well." He smoothed the fur on his cat, his straight blond hair draping over his face. "If this all goes well…" His eyes shifted, and he swallowed. "And I go back to 1946. Well, I wanted to keep an eye out for that Trek show. When will it start again?"

His eyes seemed so big and sad. I hoped at least for his and Edith's sake that things went back to normal.

"It came out, um, in 1966." I had to stop myself from saying a few years ago. "Oh, and uh, Wallace?"

"Yes?"

"Are you going to talk about the future when you get back?" I asked.

"You shouldn't," Edith said, having woken up.

"Oh, um." He took a moment to really think about this. He looked around a little sadly before saying, "That's not going to be fun."

"I agree," Edith said, rubbing her eyes.

I bit my tongue. It was their choice after all.

"Ready?" Edith asked. We both nodded with a certain stiffness.

I got into my position in the corner of the room, phaser in hand. Wallace and Edith stood in the middle. Tiny ripples of water crashed silently against my foot.

"Remember," Edith said, "no matter what happens, keep trying."

I nodded stiffly once again. I imagined I was just like Captain Kirk, saving his Enterprise and crew.

"Wait," Wallace said. "I just want to say in case this is the last time we see each other." He paused before deciding on simply, "Bye."

I felt myself smile along with Edith. "Maybe in the future," I said.

"Deal," Edith said. "If this works, anyone recognizes anyone down the line, we'll say hello."

It was a nice, if not odd, thought, since to each of us, present, future and past were three very different times. It was odd thinking about them being able to recognize me as I am, but to me they would be in their twenties and thirties. I looked at Edith one last time. If this all went according to plan, we would never know each other at the same age.

"Deal," Wallace and I said together.

I straightened my back to match Wallace's posture and turned to the mirror. I exhaled, shut my eyes, then opened them. I shot my phaser at the corner. Its light webbed out countless times over and over and over again, like a *James Bond* movie, except it was only really one line duplicated all around. I began yelling for The Magician to come. Causing it to come to us would mean we wouldn't get caught off guard. I kept my eye on the red and purple lights. It was a hypnotizing look. I could hear Wallace and Edith digging into the ground. Eventually, it should make a hole. The idea wasn't that my phaser was really doing anything. After all, it was just a shiny light, a momentary distraction, just to buy some time.

The smoke was rolling in. The thick clouds draped over the duplicated rooms with a hypnotic fog. I kept my eyes fixated on the purple and red in the mirror. I began to feel an odd sensation; I had to keep my focus. I could tell something must look different about me, because I could distantly hear Edith having to keep Wallace from looking at me, clearly bothered by something.

"Quit trying to escape, think of what you will become."

My curiosity was starting to get to me. My eyes were watery from not blinking. My finger was numb from pressing the trigger so hard. And I was feeling off, a sickly feeling was coming over me. I was really cold, like my feet were frozen in place, though I dared not look down. My head was hot, it was like swimming through mud getting myself to stay focused. It was taking everything in me to not look over at Wallace and Edith, to see their progress. How much longer had I left?

"Dean," Edith called. "Start walking over to us... But." She paused. She sounded uncomfortable. "Shut your eyes, and don't open them until I say."

I must look really different. I was abundantly aware of how Wallace was clearly stifling sobs. I wanted to look down so bad. To know just what I was dealing with here. I blinked, two fat tears streamed down my cheeks and stopped on my jaw, which in its own right had a ticklish annoyance. But I kept my eyes still.

"Now, Dean!" Edith said urgently.

I shut my eyes. It was so disconcerting not being able to see in a nightmare room.

"STOP. STAY WITH ME. YOU ARE SAFE."

The voice was yelling, but slowly, each word was focused and painful. I turned my body, moving robotically to where I had last heard Edith.

"Follow my voice... I'm here... You're doing great..." Edith's voice was farther away than I had hoped. She seemed to be fighting back emotions herself. The voice was so loud, it was drowning hers out.

"YOUR WORLD IS UNSAFE. STAY WITH ME."

I paused momentarily. Jarred in place.

"Keep walking!" Edith called, panicked by my pause.

"I WILL KEEP YOU SAFE."

My head snapped back. Eyelids taken by images. I was on a beach, I was full. I hadn't even realized how hungry I was. Looking off, the orange night sky was full of stars, multiple moons and suns. I was far away. I wasn't on Earth; I was somewhere no human has ever been. The planet had a ring around it like Saturn. This caused a gorgeous almost mirage-like view. The ring was luminescent like crushed diamonds. It cast a long crescent-shaped shadow as far as my eye could see, along the beach and gray water. I felt like I was on a well-deserved vacation for the first time in years.

"Please, Dean!" Edith's words made their way into my feverish mirage.

Her words caught me by surprise, she sounded like she was holding back tears. I looked around my own paradise, horrified. Trying to block it out.

"Open your eyes!" she screamed.

My eyelids snapped open. It was everything I had wanted to do since shutting them. The room was musky and smog-like, but I could just make Edith's form out. I ran to her, keeping my eyes only on her. Just her. Remembering not to look at whatever horrible image I must be.

"Why go to such a callous place? Please, stay."

The Magician's sad tone was almost enough to catch me off guard, it sounded hurt by our leaving.

I dropped my phaser and took Edith's hand. We plunged down into the wet clayish ground together. It felt like going down a throat that was pushing us back up. It was grossly wet. I dared not think how I was breathing. Wallace seemed farther down. I looked at Edith, fully grateful to her, but I forced our hands to let go. I saw her lips mouth the words. *"I'll look for you,"* before I crashed onto my bed.

My hands groped my covers, and then my chest with disbelief. Did our childish plan really work? I sat up and looked around my dark room. The moon was in its same position and half full or empty phase. I looked at my clock. ten forty-six p.m. If I was really back to my time, then that meant not only had no time passed but it was also a minute before.

Then I heard him. The movement outside my room. Before thinking better of it, I ran out into the hallway.

"Dean?" my brother said, forgetting he needed to whisper.

"Dennis!" I said with an overwhelming amount of emotion. I ran into his arms, snuggling my head into his stomach.

"Whoa, it's okay, buddy. You got to be quiet for me, okay?" He dropped his car keys and hugged me back. "What's all this?"

"I missed you!" I was talking without thinking, emotions and relief overtaking me.

"Sure, I missed you too, but seriously, I need you to be quiet," he said in a hushed whisper.

I sniffed. "Don't worry, I won't say a thing."

"Say what thing?" he asked. His deep-set eyes were curious.

I mentally thanked Edith and Wallace for apparently keeping

secrets better than I could.

"Never mind that, I just was scared. I thought I heard something."

"Oh." He smiled wearily. "Well, fear not, it's just me."

I smiled. I really smiled. Then I swallowed some pride. "Can I sleep in your room tonight?"

I fell asleep thinking, before exhaustion overtook me. I hoped Edith and Wallace were really okay – wherever their lives were now – and I mourned the loss of my phaser, before drifting off to sleep.

I woke up the next morning with my phaser in hand, but its batteries were terribly hot and burned-out dead.

Come and Spend the Night with Me on Halloween

Of course, I knew him before I really met him. After all, it was my job to know him. Like all my coworkers I had my doubts and my theories, but there wasn't much we could do, we didn't have enough to pin any of them for murder. Still, the cork board, pictures, and yarn were never far from his name.

At the time, I was so nervous about being caught as a police officer that I didn't think to get a good look at other people.

"Could I bum one of those?" I had plunged both hands deep within my tan jacket and walked over to the small covering he had taken from the rain. My head slightly dipped, letting the rain drops fall off my hair and miss my glasses.

He was just taller than me. He turned his head dramatically, a sort of slow 'Jimmy Stewart movie' turn. But I was dressed nicer, his dark jacket was high water on his wrists.

"Sure," he mumbled with his own cigarette still between his teeth. "Come here often?" His cigarette bobbed with his eyebrow raised and a cheeky smile, a knowing humor.

The Dive was a notorious bar among the right crowd. Nearly thirty minutes away from Wallaceville, it was the only gay bar for hundreds of miles; or at the very least it was the only gay bar I knew of up north.

"When I have time off." I took the cigarette in hand, drumming the back of it on my chest before putting it between my own teeth, so I could lean into his light. I inhaled fully, letting my head clear and my mouth dry out, then pushed my glasses up. "You?"

"The same, I figured it wouldn't be a bad place on Halloween." He grinned slightly, a toothy, almost childishly charming smile. Like he had a secret joke to himself.

"Not much fun after growing up?" I ran a hand through my wet hair. He had a young sort of look to him, maybe college-aged.

His lips dipped into a line, he turned away from me and looked to the drizzling sky. "I was thinking about getting a bite to eat, should I suppose you know a place?"

I watched as he folded the napkin over his lap, I hadn't expected this sort of manners. The place I picked out was just across the street from The Dive, a dingy twenty-four-hour breakfast place. Low lighting and a staff that knew I was a cop. Admittedly, I loved the way the rain had made our hair and the dramatic contrast we had. My hair was just a bit lighter than his, but his eyes were a dramatic light blue, whereas mine were a deep brown. We both had shoulders hunched, the cold made us lean in and talk quieter.

"So, may I ask your name?" I asked with a small, lip-parted grin.

"Ken Vallenger, the one and only." He gave a toothy charming smile.

It's moments like this where I wish I was better at my job.

My own grin faded. "Ken Vallenger?" I was barely audible, my hand gripped my side, where my gun usually was. More accurately though, I probably looked pained.

"What's the matter? Have we met?" He tipped forward in his chair, curious and eyeing me, trying to see if I was someone he knew.

Everything that seemed charming about him felt more like a ruse now. To call it a sobering moment was laughable. This scared me. It actually frightened me. I could feel the miles of wood around us, imagining my face carved on the side of a milk carton. I thought about the rain washing away evidence and footprints.

"Seriously, do we know each other?" Ken asked with his would-be innocently curious eyes.

I wasn't quite sure what to do. What to say. How to answer him. My mind had an odd drowning feel to it. Like I had stuck it in a fish tank. So, I just turned back to his face and started talking.

"I'm Aaron Teller, the current deputy of Wallaceville. Maybe you know, you've managed an infamous name for our small police force." My voice had a hollow empty sound, none of the demanding sound I ached for. Even calling myself the deputy was pretty rich, there were only three of us on the force, and I was only deputy while Mark was on paternity leave.

I watched Ken's well-maintained flirty face dip; a sort of sour expression came over him.

Sucking his cheeks to his teeth, he leaned back in his chair and crossed an arm over front. "I suppose something of the sort was bound to come up tonight, well, if I'm the unlucky one."

I had practically told the guy I thought he was a murderer, and he just deflected. "The unlucky one? That's what you call it?" My voice was still a hollow whisper.

His clear eyes squinted at me, measuring me up. "What? Don't tell me, Deputy, do you actually plan on hearing me out?"

My head was feeling oddly light, a sort of breeziness was coming over me. I momentarily wondered if this was how my head would feel bald. "I've got a free night, go ahead and tell me."

"How much do you know?" He leaned in further; his voice was a low whisper.

This was about to be too easy; it was a small town and an infamous story. "On Halloween 1950, you, your sister Eve, and two friends, Randy and Jo Hedgecomb, found the body of Terrence O'Mally. On Halloween 1951, you and Randy discovered the body of Jean White. On Halloween 1952, you and Randy watched Alicia Marsh get hit by a car. On Halloween 1953, your sister Eve found Eric Lane's body. In 1954, Randy and Jo—"

"I understand." Ken cut me off. "So, you know that between me, and my sister, Randy and Jo, have each found a dead body on Halloween since 1950."

"Yes," I said, even nodding slightly. Truthfully, a part of me was expecting to fall over dead just talking to him on Halloween.

"Between us, we have found seven bodies in a row." His voice carried no discerning emotion. He pressed his lips to his drink and took a loud gulp, his Adam's apple bobbing.

"So, eight after tonight," I spoke before thinking.

His eyebrows went up and his gaze met mine, then he turned to put his glass down and nodded himself. "Yeah, I s'pose eight tonight."

I swallowed hard, my throat felt thick, coated in wax. "You called yourself unlucky. Is that all? That's all you're calling it?"

"What do you call it?" His voice crept up to an edge.

"Well." I swallowed again. "It's—it's a bit odd."

"Odd?" He quoted my lame remark back at me.

"Yeah." I swallowed again. "Unlucky just doesn't seem to cover it."

"So, I should say it's been odd, not unlucky?" He took another loud gulp of his drink.

"Well, Edward Winter, the Sheriff—" I started.

"We've met."

"Right, sorry. Edward seems to think—"

"That I, or we, had something to do with it? Right?"

I swallowed again. "Not exactly, he just finds it—"

"A bit odd," Ken finished. "Look, I realize you think you're on a date with Dracula. Or maybe just a murderer with an affinity with Halloween, or that I want you to be body number eight." He shrugged his shoulders, and leaned in closer. "Or, do you plan on hearing me out?"

There was something in him laying the cards out on the table like that. It brought something back to me; it didn't make me braver. It compelled me. I sat up a bit straighter, and took my jacket off, laying it on the booth. "I will, but I want more than just you saying it's unlucky."

Ken smiled, a humorless sort of smile. "I'll tell you what I know. But you're going to find that that's all there is to it. I'm just not a very lucky guy."

1950 – Ken

"Wait," Jo called. "Let's do the houses over the bridge then call it a night."

"If our mothers heard you now." Randy shook his head in a slow, floppy way, reminiscent of his dad, but he had a sly grin that was nothing like Mr. Hedgecomb.

I agreed. The houses over the bridge were certainly nice, the type to have full candy bars, but they were also surrounded by forest and out of the way. Our parents finding out would be in poor taste.

"You're not going to tell, right?" Jo asked, her teeth clamped together, and her hair growing spiky from the humidity (which just added to her witch look).

"I won't!" Eve was bouncing on her heels, her cat ears

bobbing.

"Let's do it," I agreed, realizing they couldn't see my smile as a ghost.

I was quickly deemed the leader of the path since my costume was the easiest to follow in the dark. We were going to have to move quickly if we were going to catch the houses with their lights still on.

"This is going to be hard to explain," Randy said in a haughty sort of voice, lifting up his leg to show the mud caked on his once-white shoes.

"Just shuffle your feet across the bridge," Jo told him.

I had always liked the bridge, it was the sort of thing my mom called handsome; shiny stones with child-height low bars, as if it was out of some sort of gothic fairytale of a haunted bridge meant for children. Once I stepped foot on the ancient thing, I immediately switched over to scooting my shoes, hoping the black stone would scrape the dirt off.

Without much vision, both from the dark and my sheet ghost costume, I made out each person reaching the bridge by sound. The way our shoes scraped across the bridge. The sound of me alone, then getting followed by a second, third, and fourth dirty pair of shoes. I imagined how idiotic we must have looked. A costumed kid parade that only made shuffling noises.

In truth, I was too focused on my own feet. Maybe I would have never noticed if I was alone.

It was Eve who saw it first that year.

Her scream was so immediate, so all-encompassing. A sort of shattering sound. I shut my eyes before thinking about turning. But I needed the noise to stop. I turned so quickly my ghost costume billowed around me like a ballgown.

Her white hand pointed over the small rail. I must have

dropped my pillowcase because all I could think to do was pull her small body into a hug before following her gaze.

"Oh, wow," Jo said to my left.

"I'm going to be sick," Randy whispered. I could hear his feet moving to the other side of the bridge, and the retching sounds coming from deep within his chest. That sort of full-body need.

I fruitlessly covered my sister's eyes. She didn't protest, she just breathed heavily into my arm.

My ghost costume tunnel-vision gave me a weird spotlight of the body.

His arms and legs seemed swollen. I wasn't just seeing a white leg, but pale muscle peeled back, and bone poked through. Almost like a grotesque water lily. His jaw was slack in an inhuman way and had a whole mop of mud-caked dirty hair. Half of his body was sunk under the muddy water, like a shallow bath. In fact, even if the mud and rain hadn't done a number on him, the mangled way he was lying, and pale complexion gave away that he was no longer with the living.

None of us asked each other if we were really seeing a dead guy, because we knew, even at our age. Only magic shows and movies could try to sell us that this figure could stand up again. Even with the minimal black and white death we had been allowed to see on TV, just seeing this in color would have been a nightmare. But this wasn't fake, it wasn't makeup, and it definitely wasn't a movie.

Randy's 5th Avenue puke reached the figure, mixing and discoloring his shallow grave.

The phrase 'washing downstream' came to my mind as I watched the brown chunks ruin the already ruined form.

"We need to go home." My words came out cotton-mouthed,

even more than a whisper, I was nearly silent.

We all got dirty, but this time we didn't mind. We walked haphazardly, aware of our movements. Each of us had removed parts of our costumes. My sheet ghost costume was wrapped around Eve. Jo and Randy had removed their witch and pirate hats, which had a pledge of allegiance, or more accurately, funeral feel about it. I sweaty-palmed carried mine and Eve's candy and led the pack again, feeling the dirt stick to and cake on my ankles.

Once back in our own neighborhood, only a smattering of older kids was still out, and only now did I realize how dark it was. Somehow no one seemed to be looking over. Like we were some invisible group of child ghosts.

I walked up the steps of my house feeling a strong wave of tiredness. The way my dad ached coming back from the run he went on once a month. Feeling my full sight back, but none of the clarity. Was I really the boy who had left this house?

Eve stood just behind me, looking cold with the discolored white sheet wrapped around her, her hair plastered to her cheeks, cat ears crooked, and her eyes locked on the floor. Seeing her like this weirdly annoyed me.

Randy and Jo stayed at the bottom of the steps, acting as if they weren't invited inside. Still holding onto their candy bags and hats, looking ready to share the good word or deliver the bad news.

"C'mon in." I broke the silence we had been holding onto. "My mom will understand."

But once I saw my mom's face, something broke in me. Or maybe something was fully realized. At that moment, I remembered that I wasn't an adult. That I really was just some kid. My eyes flooded, tears brimming over instantly.

"What is it, Ken?" My mom grabbed my shoulders, I was struck. Had I ever noticed the way her caramel-colored eyes really listened. She crouched down to my height, her eyebrows pinched together as she looked at all of us.

"The thing is," I started, aware of what I really was going to say, "we saw something…"

After I finished, my mom paced around the room. She went over to the wooden end table and took a big gulp of her tea, then in a sort of sleep-walking way, handed her teacup to me as she called the police.

I looked down at my reflection in the brown Earl Gray, then decided and took a swig of the bitter drink. I dropped the cup, running to the bathroom to throw up.

1957 – Aaron

His drink was drained. "Then I slept in my mom's room after Sheriff Winter left." I nodded.

Ken's eyes refocused, having gotten lost in his story, seeing my face. His eyebrows pinched together, not sympathetically, more a bitter curiosity. "What's wrong, Aaron?"

"Nothing," I said lamely. "I get your point, I didn't really know. I knew the names, and the date, and the years, but I didn't know."

Ken now gave me a small honest smile, not happy, but a sober understanding. "I didn't murder anyone as a kid, or as a teenager, or now as an adult." He pushed a hand through his now dry hair.

"I'm not saying I really believed that," I started. "Or Sheriff Edward for that matter. But why? I mean, why Halloween? Why you? It's not even like every year was the exact same type of death." My questions were rhetorical, aimed at the world, or some prophet – whatever caused these things.

"What do you mean?"

"Well, take 1952, I mean you saw her—"

"I don't want to talk about her," Ken interrupted me.

"I'm sorry, I wasn't thinking." Now I shifted my gaze to look out the water-stained window. I remembered reading that the little girl had been dressed as Snow White, but now that I was talking to Ken, I also remembered Edward telling me Ken was holding the body when he pulled his police cruiser up. Ken had watched the car hit her.

"That's why I said we're just unlucky," Ken said, and I turned back. "You're right in saying it's odd, it's certainly that, but I don't think it can be thought about normally."

"What? Like a curse?"

"I don't know. That's probably the best word for it." Ken leaned his head up to the ceiling, almost lazily. "I don't know if I believe in much. I haven't had any interesting deals with the devil. I suppose I was a bad person in my previous life. Maybe this is my hell. Maybe we walked on a haunted bridge. It's all noise and speculation and it all just comes back to me knowing that October 31st is far from my lucky day."

Our tired waitress began placing our food down. Ken sat up again and gave her a charming smile and a truthful 'thanks' before she left. It was jarring, Ken was sort of miserable to watch.

"And here I was hoping you could take my mind off things." Ken laughed a low chuckle to himself.

I chuckled too. "That's my bad, sorry."

"I'll chalk it up to an occupational hazard." He waved his fork. "And anyway, you might get to be sorrier." Ken's tongue was picking at a bottom tooth as he moved his wrist forward to check the time. "Halloween's not over. Have you ever seen a dead body, Deputy?"

I nodded. "Yeah, my dad's." I kept my eyes on my food and pushed my mashed potatoes around a bit.

Ken's head shot up; I could feel his eyes on me. "Ah jeez. Look, Aaron, I'm sorry."

I looked up and smiled. "Think nothing of it, my dad was starting to ask about me finding a wife. I'm sure the relationship wouldn't be cordial today."

We started to eat in mostly silence, even enjoying some small talk. The rain would pick up and die down, then start up again. After I paid for the check, I met him outside enjoying another cigarette.

"Maybe it was lucky I met you, Deputy." Ken took a deep inhale, his eyes half closed, savoring it.

"Why is that?" I plunged my hands deep into my pockets again.

"I s'pose having a cop as a friend could come in handy." He winked. Then we walked back to his place.

The way the night was going, I can't say I was exactly shocked. Boy, would it have been bad had we not asked for each other's names. Talk about a double whammy.

If asked, I might have believed the body would be the thing to haunt me, the image or face of my nightmares. That's the idea, right? If you find a dead body, that should be the thing talked about, that's the whole point.

But now I knew the way Ken knew.

In truth, the body was real, it existed. Terms like rigor mortis, and decomposition, came into my head. But the thing that really haunted me was turning to look back at Ken.

It was because he wasn't screaming in panic. That John Ford

cowboy.

In fact, had I not known better, I would have said he seemed happy, but I did know better; he was relieved. As if his expression could say, 'now that that's over, maybe I can go to sleep.'

"I'll have to give Edward a call." I gripped the hair on the back of my neck.

"That sounds all right, I'll call the guys and let them know it was me."

After 1957, every year I would meet up with Ken and spend Halloween with him. I had heard of cat and mouse games. But this was different. Ken was hardly a criminal; I was just a cop coming early to a crime scene.

I wished that was the end of our story.

In truth, the third-party friend group was always the background noise I should have paid attention to. Ken talked about them, explained that the group believed that if they spread out, the cops couldn't pin them all.

But they knew it could frame one of them.

After that first night, I agreed with Ken – it was just unlucky. An annoying answer at best.

But I forgot to think about the way death changes a person. With Ken, I kept an eye on him. I knew it was the least I could do after the year we met. Spending the night on Halloween was a ritual, more than a friendly gesture. I tried to share, shoulder, some of that pain that had been forced on him.

Randy visited in 1960, played cards, and watched *The Twilight Zone* with us. In truth, I thought it sounded fun, even if just a bit odd. I agreed with Ken that speculation was hardly needed, but perhaps, 'having entered The Twilight Zone,' was a pretty good answer.

At eight p.m. we were walking Randy back out to his car.

The well-combed red leaves placed in various piles around the park suited it wonderfully. The smatterings of cherry red on the ground were making up for the balding look of the trees. I fully inhaled the bitter smell of Ken's cigarette, enjoying it mixed with the cold air.

"You see that," Randy said. I turned to his face first before letting my eyes flicker to where he was pointing.

Of course, this was no fun. Even when you expect to see these things, it still sucks. But even so, we still stood there with hands in our pockets and heads slightly turned down. Ken didn't even drop his cigarette. We looked as if Randy was pointing to a particularly nice dandelion.

It was obvious that this was the handiwork of someone who had wanted her to die, which wasn't good – not that it's ever good, but, if you're the type of person to find a body anyway...

Eventually, the body isn't the problem, it's how much it looks like you could have had something to do with it.

How odd.

The logistics of dumping a body here. Of all places.

The leaves had been raked into their handsome crimson piles at midday. So, someone found a window of time in the past four hours to dump her here?

Now I really looked at the body, the way it was laid out, how perfectly propped up it was. The woman was older, but it was obvious this wasn't a person who had died of a heart attack in public.

Like we had all seen before, she was pale, and outrageously relaxed-looking. But she really didn't look as if she had been dead for very long.

"What's the matter, Officer?" Randy asked with a light sense of humor.

I don't know if it was his tone of voice, or even if it was because we were on the way to his car, but something about this shifted. Like a truth told as a lie.

"What is this? What have you done?" The questions spilled out of my lips. My hands gripped each other, a self-comforting gesture. I could feel the anger bubbling under.

"Aaron—" Ken grabbed my wrist; he had a calming sort of tone. But even his pale eyes turned to Randy.

Randy's freakishly calm eyes.

"C'mon?" Randy posed; his voice moved up an octave.

I didn't want to be right, but if I wasn't right? Man, oh man was I going to look like the bad guy. "We'll call Edward." I turned to look at Ken. "But I just want to ask him a few questions. If he really had nothing to do with it, then there shouldn't be any problem."

Ken – 1960

"He said she was in poor health."

"Jesus, how the fuck did he know that?"

"He saw her leave a cancer support group." Aaron exhaled fully; the smoke made my eyes water. "Could I have another? I'll need to call Edward again."

"Yeah." My voice was soft, hollow. I gave him the pack.

I walked back to the kitchen where Randy was cuffed to the radiator. I knew we weren't the sheet ghost and pirate that we were ten years ago. But still. Hadn't he been the one to puke?

"Your boyfriend's pretty good at his job, I thought it'd take him longer to figure it out." Randy had his head against the white tiles, eyes closed, sitting awfully casual for my liking.

"Why?" The question was childish.

His amber eyes pinched together in the first really real way that night. "Did you notice the time?"

"What?"

"It's past midnight." His lips separated, making a soft smile. "No one died." Something clicked. Maybe more likely, something broke.

"What?"

"We found ten bodies by accident, this one we found on purpose." Randy crossed his leg over one another. "We didn't find a body by accident this year."

I should have said 'what' again, but instead my jaw went slack. I just stood there with my mouth gaping at him.

"I did what was too scary to even ask, let alone do. I don't know why, or what we did. But it sets us apart from the world. Your boyfriend can come over and pretend he's a part of this too. But this was our world, our problem. What if this stopped it? Ken, no one else died." He ran a hand through his hair, looking relieved. "Yeah, I did that, I really understand, okay? But maybe next year no one will die? I'm hopeful for that."

I had heard of desperate moves, bold moves, even opportunism, but this? Randy really believed that if he took matters literally into his own hands, maybe he had broken it, put a stop to this?

Yes. Of course, I wanted an end. I wanted it more than anything. I never dared dream because of it all. I loved Aaron. But he didn't really know. But I believed Eve knew. Jo knew. Randy.

My mouth pooled with saliva, and my brain dared to never give me a night of sleep again.

My stomach had dropped, just fallen through the floorboards. I felt the pain deep in my knee before I realized that

65

my legs were shaking. I just sat on the floor. I plugged my ears; if he talked more, I didn't want to hear it. I was so tired. So exhausted by the world.

I thought of Alicia Marsh, the way she was so instantly taken from the world, how her blood ruined her gold Snow White skirt. I hoped, needed, to believe that her brain gave her silence in the end. Maybe in time I will share Randy's optimism for next Halloween, maybe I already shared his madness. With all this noise in my head.

It's horrifically amazing, I try, but I can't remember a time when I actually enjoyed Halloween. For all I am, and all I can remember, Halloween has always scared me.

A Terrible Night, What a View, a Gust of Wind for Me and You

It had been nearly a week since I had been spitting blood and drowning, but still, going back to work was bound to happen eventually. I was shifting my armpit against my crutch when my eyebrows turned up to his image across the computerized billboard screen. My face felt hot, even to a comedic extent. Calm down, man, no one knows. Of course, except for him.

It seemed outrageous to me now, even obvious, that the most important thing to ever happen to me, had been happenstance. That I really am only as interesting as my experiences.

Even at the start, we knew.

Everyone had a self-knowing, roll-the-eyes type tone when they said it. Superhero. I almost would have thought that with a decent gallery of comic books and novels, we could have come up with a better name for him. Nevertheless, he graduated from 'The Man in the Mask' to 'The Masked Man'.

The Masked Man had the whole nine yards: a color-coded costume, online debate over whether or not he was some rich guy with a ton of gadgets, or some guy who, somehow, happened to get superhuman abilities.

There were even rumors that the government was looking into what could have caused him. Investigations into radioactive power plants, chemical spills and mishaps, and what household items could do to the human body, besides just kill you.

In truth, even I had a few weeks where I was at least looking the guy up – but everyone did, at least at some point. For me, I think it was because he was in my city. That was enough to make it more personal. A way to make my daily commute at least slightly more interesting. I'd look up to the sky on occasion, or turn my head in excitement, if I heard a loud noise.

At first, the Masked Man had broken up petty crime then graduated to a few more newsworthy criminals. The public opinion started off positive, excited that something so novelistic had made its way to real life – it was enough to garner some fame. After all, there was something to having mundane crime solved theatrically.

The Masked Man figured out his branding or understood what a real-life comic book should entail. Typically, the culprit would be found strung up by just black duct tape, with his name written in white ink along the crotch. Dangling in front of the police station, ripe for the taking and red faced.

Not to say it was all fun. It seemed this Masked Man could only make individual aspects of crime feel resolved, not actual crime rates (which were actually on the rise). Making it a true self-fulfilling prophecy that our city would now not only attract crime, but more colorful criminals at that.

Even after all that, my own thoughts on the vigilante hero had eventually been overwhelmingly mild; at most, the guy operated as only background noise in my life. Like everyone else, I had my own problems to worry about. The day I saw him was different though.

I was on the subway towards my apartment after a long day at the office, twenty-four years old and like most good kids my age, I already had settled for jobs I didn't want.

My eyes were fixated on the overhead light reflecting on the shifting walls. Absentmindedly daydreaming about what I could do at home that would make the day not a total waste.

I didn't even hear the cause of the crash.

An awful screeching noise that was so loud I could only fixate on clapping my hands to my head and squeezing my eyes shut.

The tram stopped so suddenly I was thrown on my front, knocking the wind out of my chest. Then the tram started tipping over.

I was going down with the ship. I opened my eyes and childishly extended both my arms, like I was signaling to the wall to not hit me.

My eyes steamed open with tears when my calves hit the seats on the left-hand side. I had hit them hard enough to know that I needed to grope around for blood, and maybe bone.

It took me another moment to register that I was wet. My blood trailed my eyes to the inky papers, mixing the red blood with blue ink.

The tram was now on its left side, off the tracks, and filling up with water.

"It's so not my day," I said under my breath, as I threw my wet hair back with my right hand and with my left, I gripped the hot blood below my knee.

My boring life was getting rocked with the idea that my leg was not my biggest worry.

I gripped the icy metal seats that had ruined my legs and focused on pulling myself up, favoring my right side. My mind raced as I looked around the fully sideways tram, scanning for a way out, before registering that my glasses had fallen off. I made out the black rims floating away from me and waddled my way over.

My legs were both in bad shape and walking through water

didn't help. Like an old man, I cursed loudly in mental preparation before bending down to grab my glasses.

Standing in the sideways cart I was aware that as a kid I had enjoyed the idea of a sideways or upside-down room. Admittedly, if I wasn't about to drown it would have been pretty cool.

I scanned hard for an escape. The window in the farthest left corner above me – now the roof – was shattered.

So, I waited.

It didn't take long for the cold water to reach my neck. Now at the halfway point of the tram, I had only minutes, surely, and I would safely climb out, find a way down, and limp my way home.

A pathetically sad way to end the night. But also, too good to be true.

Another loud, horribly high-pitched sound, halfway between a scream and a screech, echoed around the walls. Followed by the sounds of creaking metal and glass breaking.

Ruining my fantasy of an easy escape, I whipped my head around wildly, expecting to be able to look out the window and see some monstrosity, but the windows now made up the floor and ceiling of the car. My teeth clamped together, and I half hoped I would actually just drown.

After a long and painful minute, my head was starting to get up to the broken window, cursing what had to be the unluckiest day of my life.

I shut my eyes and then gripped either end of the broken window. Inhaling deeply, I shut my eyes. Mentally preparing before making my move out. My hands were getting torn by glass, but I swiftly moved myself halfway up and leaned my stomach against the side.

What I did see was almost too much to take in.

Children's books dreamed of having a monster this scary. The best way to describe it was a bat gone wrong. But calling it a bat was generous. Even horrific vampires didn't look like this bat. It was the size of a car and had monstrously distorted facial features and body, white creamy eyes and grayish teeth that dripped some awful chunky pink liquid. It was crouched down on top of another turned subway car, scanning the room with its milky eyes.

Before I could think of being quiet, I had already gritted my teeth and grunted and sloshed water violently by getting up.

Its head had snapped in my direction and its solid creamy eyes seemed to have focused onto me.

I really should have drowned when I had the chance.

I cut my hands painfully and deeper on the broken window as I squirmed rapidly, trying to get out. I could only see flashes – like my brain could only operate like a strobe light. My clumsy, wet, bleeding hands flailing for anything to grip.

The creature was coming towards me, crawling, its wet wings flapping without flight. It was drenching the walls with water and snapping its mouth.

The Masked Man?

A sudden light but clear creaking sound was made as the young and fit hero smashed his feet down onto the car.

"Whoa, you are ugly. I can't wait to see what sort of vat of chemicals or military project spilled onto you." A wonderful alto voice called out and laughed to himself. There he was – the black, blue and red skintight suited man.

I paused my movement, leaning painfully against the broken window. Like being caught in headlights, I couldn't help but take him in.

Tall and lean, sounding young in age, but certainly beyond

human in ability. Calling it flying wasn't quite right – the way he moved seemed to have earned its online debates. He moved like a swinging Tarzan, but it was unclear what caused this. His hands seemed clenched, but I couldn't make out wires or anything physically causing this.

My sore eyes broke away from the fight to take in the room. Broken pipes along the wall were flooding the room with water, nothing past the ankles on the ground, but I could see how my poorly placed car had filled up so quickly. Three subway cars, including my own, had been flipped or turned from the sudden stop. Anyone unlucky enough to have been here at this late hour, had already left in a hurry.

The Masked Man swung forward and aimed a hit on the middle of the bat's face, where a nose would have been. The monster landed hard on its back, the Masked Man's strength also living up to its inhuman ability.

The bat screeched another long, horrible sound. I gasped audibly.

For a moment I saw The Masked Man turn towards me, a quick glance, then turn back to the monster to dodge a hit from the wide wing coming towards him.

"All right, big boy, you're making my grade school Halloween costume look like I wasn't even trying." He laughed to himself once again, only in a deeper tone, then proceeded to do a backflip and grabbed a pipe from the wall, spraying more water all over the subway.

Another loud, angry screech. But the pause had cost the monster; the Masked Man slammed the pipe deep into the creature's wide, screaming mouth, stabbing its tongue and carving the pipe clear through the side of the monster's cheek.

The monster wailed something horrible. The sound was

enough that I had to focus on not passing out. Even with glasses my vision blurred. Gripping the edge of the window with wet slippery fingertips.

The monster bent over in pain, and with his foot, the Masked Man lazily pushed the monster off the subway.

As a final goodbye, the monster landed his first hit on him. A claw from his wing slashed along the Masked Man's neck down to his side. Although not a deep cut, the suit cut open, allowing just the smallest peek at his well-defined neck and shoulder.

"Ah, great." He sighed, back to a more alto-sounding voice.

I began to move myself up more, crawling on the slippery glass, annoyed now that I could fully feel how cold the water really was.

I didn't even hear him come over.

"Let's get you home, before the vampire bat wakes up." His voice was now back to being a deeper tone.

"Right." I couldn't think of what to say. My life really had gone unusual. He seemed to be abnormally strong for his slim size as he gripped my scarlet stained hand and pulled me out of the water, placing me down steadily on the side of the subway car.

"Ah." He inhaled sharply and grabbed his revealed left shoulder, which was bleeding ever so slightly.

"Looks like we both need to get home," I said with a forced airy tone.

He laughed once in a deep tone. "You more so than me." His masked eyes seemed to be traversing over my injuries. "Well, if you're comfortable with it, go ahead and climb on my back."

"What?"

He laughed. "Look, dude, I've got to hide the rip in the suit and your leg looks pretty bad. But I guess if you prefer walking home…" He made a move as if to wave goodbye and I caught his wrist.

Who knew a near death experience could make me so bold? I was as surprised as he was as we both turned to my hand on his wrist.

Before I could think of apologizing, he laughed, now in a more alto-sounding tone. "Now you're thinking." He moved my wrist to his exposed shoulder.

"All right, now hold on tight," he said.

I clasped my bleeding hands together and locked my bleeding legs around his waist. I was almost feeling secure when he jumped.

My eyes instinctively drooped, and my stomach dropped. Sure, he seemed in control of what was happening, but I couldn't figure out how.

My stomach ached something awful and I buried my face in his shoulder, shutting my eyes. Now feeling the full weight of what had happened to me, not only in the past hour, but how I was even remotely going to process what was currently happening.

"All right, tell me how to get you home before you throw up."

"I'm not going to throw up," I said, only mildly annoyed as I opened my eyes. To my surprise, I was much closer to my apartment building than I thought. "Oh, my apartment is that black one on the corner down there." I gripped his chest tightly as I pointed in the direction I wanted. A single drop of blood from my hand fell, left to fly in the air and hit the pavement like rain.

"Next to the laundromat?" He shifted his eyes to mine momentarily. "Your glasses are going to need to be fixed," he commented, then traced the crack with his finger.

Wow, I thought. I hoped he couldn't tell how in love with him

I was. "Yeah, that's the one."

"Awesome."

Then he changed the way he was gripping his left hand and jumped, actually jumping in mid-air, as if the air beneath him was solid.

"Oh jeez," I said as we landed on the roof of the nearest building.

"Okay now I can tell where you live." He sounded relieved.

"Wait, now you know which apartment I live in?" My eyebrows shot up.

Even through the mask I could tell he was trying to figure out how best to put this particular power. "Yeah, it's sorta like an occupational hazard, I can like…" He shifted his eyes for a moment. "Smell it."

"Oh my gosh!" I exclaimed and then laughed harder than I had in months.

"We're about five buildings away, and it smells nice so don't worry about it, all right?"

I laughed. We were mid jump between buildings. In a moment, I felt my hair fly up, my glasses barely jumped above the bridge of my nose, and my clothing dried a little more.

Before, my stomach would have dropped; now, I focused on the city view, the sound of the wind, and how close I felt to him. I almost hoped that he could make time go a little slower and make this night last a little longer.

He climbed down to my apartment sideways, I savored the view one last time, and marveled at how it seemed even gravity couldn't make him fall. We went through my studio apartment window, and he placed me down on the floor of my apartment.

"Tell me you have some first aid stuff for your legs and hands," he said, crouching at my window, staring at my blood on his chest, his feet at the bottom and his hands holding the sides, neither in my apartment or out.

"Yeah, no worries," I said with a yawn, trying to make this whole thing sound casual. "I've got stuff for tonight and I'll go to the doctor's tomorrow."

"Well, that's a relief. I'd hate for something to happen to a nice guy like you." Even through the mask, I felt like I was hearing a softer, alto-voiced side of him.

"Well, uh, I just want to say—"

I was halfway through thanking him when it happened.

A gust of wind came strong and hard. At first, the flap of the mask where the creature had cut him flipped up, but before he could grab the flap to pull it back down, his whole mask came off.

To call it jarring was an understatement. Hell, to call it awkward would be an understatement.

He had dark, almost pitch-black hair, wet and sweaty. His face was pale and angular, he looked like he was just a few years older than me, dark tired circles under his pale eyes. He didn't even look dirty, just some blood on his ear and a little water left over from the subway was all that showed his alter-ego.

He was dead quiet. Our eyes stiffly locked together and neither of us dared to breathe. His pale blue eyes and dark eyebrows couldn't go up any higher. He was shocked, his secret identity just blew away in an instant.

And here I was, seeing what a regular guy he was. Well, a regular hot guy, with an odd job.

"I, uh—" He started talking now in whispers, almost high pitched. "Well, I'm just going to—" And then he was gone.

I stuck my head out the window in nearly every direction and never saw as much of a shadow. Even my typically busy street seemed quiet, now more focused on the sirens I could hear by the subway entrance, where it seemed every human but me and him were at right now.

Now on my way to work looking at his masked image on the billboard, I felt outrageously embarrassed. I now know the face of one of the Internet's icons. A man literally named 'The Masked Man'. Something he clearly didn't want me to know.

One photo of him carrying me home had made one news site, and it was blurry and hard to make out. It seemed even I had gone through the whole thing with my identity intact.

Nearly every other site was more worried about whatever the bat monster had been. Officially becoming The Masked Man's newest controversy, and another thing making him closer to a comic book-turned-real-life hero. My involvement was akin to just another girl (boy in my case) getting saved and carried away by the hero.

It had been nearly a week. Realistically speaking, I was aware that my experience was a one-time deal. Fifty years from now, I would think of that night as clearly as it had happened, and the only reason he would think of me is because of a gust of wind.

I dropped my keys on the counter of my sad apartment and was relieved to finally be able to eat something and rest my legs.

I had just made it to my bed when I heard, "Okay if I come in?"

The alto voice was enough for me to feel like I was turning in slow motion and for my heart to swell in a way I didn't know was possible.

The Orange Knight

"Sir, sir!" Markus yelled while shaking me awake. Almost instantly, I was propped up on my elbow – typically, I was slow to get up, but I seemed to know in my marrow that something was terribly wrong. My overgrown hair parted my vision but even through the blond slits, I could see Markus leaning over my four-poster bed. He was inhumanly pale and set in his worry.

"What's happened?"

He paused for a fraction before telling me, "It's Kurt, he's missing."

I slung my pointed arrowhead back and let it rip almost silently to the target. Piercing itself through the second ring, I exhaled and silently was pleased with myself because I knew Kurt was watching and the last thing he needed was for me to gloat. Kurt had a look in his baby blue eyes, and his jaw clenched in a new emotion for my brother – jealousy.

His arrowheads were, of course, rubber. He should have known better than to get his hopes up for the real thing. In fact, it stung in a weird way for him to be jealous of me.

"Nicely done," Kurt said. He stood tall and really seemed to be trying to give me some respect, but the sadness stayed in his blue eyes.

I wished I could teach him about how to swallow jealousy. But maybe I needed to learn a bit more myself since I was clearly getting a small amount of joy from watching him experience it.

I was my brother's back-up, and our younger sister was mine. Kurt was going to be king in under a decade when our father stepped down. I had learned pretty quickly to occupy myself with other things when Kurt was given invites to soirees and had the more interesting classes of politics and studying the lands. At times, I wished I was a commoner, so the throne would be completely out of reach, almost a background noise, instead of belonging to my fragile older brother. Always just out of arm's reach. Something I would inherit for a few years when I was elderly, if my brother didn't have any kids (which he would).

So, the whole country was his. It was annoying that he had the audacity to be jealous of me for having a pointy arrowhead. I understood why, but I also thought he was smart enough to know that I should be the one looking at him the way he was looking at me.

Rima's tiny arrow pierced through the black center, and Kurt turned around and went inside.

Although it seems like the sort of thing I would have cemented into my memory – the moment I knew my job was to be second to my brother, that I would live my entire life as a second place ribbon – that really was something I must have always known, because no crushing memory of realization kept me up at night. Really, the moment I knew I was invisible was the day we found out my brother was sick.

Kurt fell back onto his behind while I threw my head back and laughed. When I looked back at him, I could already see the tears forming in his deep-set blue eyes. He huffed out his pain in such a wimpy way it seemed to me that any outsider would have thought I was the older one. However, the point stayed that he was eleven and I was eight, but I was taller and more agile any day of the week.

I didn't realize Rima was there until I turned, and she punched me square in the nose. She was all of six and none of the strength to back up a move like that but had a helluva lot of nerve.

"Apologize, Ansal," she said sternly. What annoyed me was she was acting like my least favorite nanny, Nanny August. Puffing out her chest and turning her nose up, clearly so entranced with following the rules.

"What for?" Now I sounded whiny, or at least nasally, rubbing my nose. "We were sparring."

"You didn't have to push like that," Kurt said. Kurt was brushing the petals off his pants. He seemed to have cleared away his tears and was back to acting superior (which tended to be when I no longer wanted to hang out with him).

Kurt's fall had ruined a small corner of the flowerbeds and he had taken out one of the prongs in the crochet field. The groundskeepers weren't going to be too happy with me on that one; but I had a feeling that Kurt and Rima would make sure if the groundskeepers didn't scorch earth with me, they would.

But then Kurt turned around.

I was aware of Rima cupping her hands to her mouth. It was Kurt though, the moment or single image that haunted my dreams for years, that I had to work to remove from my memory. It was how Kurt was turned awkwardly, trying to look down his own back that was drenched in blood.

"Oh," Kurt whispered.

Sure, I had pushed him, but I had pushed him before without this kind of response. How could the bottom half of his day shirt and khaki pants have this much blood?

I was seeing everything that was happening, but it seemed almost slower or covered in ice. I knew when someone moved, or something was said, but it would take me a moment to register.

Rima's huge eyes were horrified, but also taken by curiosity. She walked over to him and lifted his shirt, a sort of child instinct taking over. A long thin gash was across his lower back.

Kurt was still turned awkwardly, taken by his own injury. "Doesn't it hurt?" Rima looked up into his eyes.

"I guess a little," he said, cocking his head to one side, really trying to consider her question, to make sense of the pool of blood. Kurt then took off his full shirt, looking at the now half white, half red shirt that dripped onto the pristine grass. "But not like this."

We each seemed frozen in place from fear, but I really felt rooted by guilt. It just didn't seem real, there was no way I had hit him that hard. I backed away, but once I had gotten my feet to move it had broken the ice – I turned and ran.

Kurt, even at his most scared, called after me.

But I ran. Really running hard. My face was streaming down tears and sweat, both burned my eyes, but I kept my feet moving.

Once I got to the back porch, I saw them next to the roses, Markus next to Nanny August.

"Markus! August!" I screamed, crying even harder. My guilt seemed to be seeping out of me. Their pairs of wide eyes and summer heat carved into me.

Waiting outside Kurt's room with Rima was hard work. The worried nannies and guards at least had something to do with plying us with lemonade, but all I and Rima could do was sit and wait.

Although Kurt's superiority and calmness made for boring games, in an odd way it made the stress of what was wrong with him a little better. It seemed no matter what, he was the best of us. Someone that calm during a crisis really was bred for a kingdom.

But that moment, the moment of Kurt awkwardly twisting, trying to look down his bloody back was always what I thought of when I thought of the moment I knew there was a line between Kurt and me. That he was more important, more fragile. That it meant more if he was hurt.

"Ansel! My gosh, Ansel, wake up!"

I propped myself up on my elbows that dug angrily into my sheets. Rubbing my tired eyes. My silk sheets hung off my waist. My room was almost too dark to adjust to, until I turned and saw Kurt ghoul-lighted by a candle. It had been hours since I had left him staring at his bloody shirt. Now Kurt was bandaged tightly around his mid-section, almost mummy-like. His deep-set eyes seemed even more tired, but he seemed his normal self.

"Kurt!" I shifted to sit up and almost leaned in to hug him, but worried I better not make anything worse. Scared to hurt him worse. I grasped my hands together awkwardly instead. "Are you… are you okay?"

Kurt exhaled. It was the way our dad did when someone whispered bad news in his ear during dinner. He gripped my four-poster bed curtain and used it to lift himself onto my bed. It was moments like this where I was even more aware of how he was shorter than me.

"Doctor Vera says I have Lyropothis." He exhaled. "Normally, it doesn't show up until the person's older." He paused and looked up. I did too but didn't see what he did.

"I bleed more than the average person when I get hurt, I also don't feel pain near as bad." He paused again, now looking down at his foot. "I can't spar with you anymore." Now he looked at me. "Dad said my body is to be protected, not something to be gambled away on childhood games."

He said it with a level of a mocking tone. Each of us kids knew our dad was not a softhearted man, he was bred for a kingdom, like his mother before him had to ingrain into him, and her father before her. We all respected him, even if we did not particularly feel love for him.

"I'm so sorry, Kurt." I suddenly felt an overwhelming feeling of not only guilt, but that I should have been the one with this Lyropothis sickness. My brother was supposed to be the strong king. I, however, had known and accepted that I was intended to be more disposable.

He exhaled again. "Don't be silly, Ansel." He gripped my shoulder. "It's good we found out with a cut this size and not from a bigger wound. I should be thanking you." It was moments like this (despite his height and occasional wimpiness) that it was clear he was the older one.

Despite his maturity, his shockingly blue eyes showcased the fear and freshness of this news on his face.

I got an idea. "Let's read the story of Knighthood Gems."

It was my brother and mine's favorite of the stories read to us. It was a children's fable about these three knights who each were to protect a kingdom.

One day, an Oracle told them that they could each have all the power they ever wanted if they could reach a faraway tower and swim out with their corresponding-colored gem. The green knight was the good knight, the orange knight was the evil knight, and the white knight was an older and more tired knight who decided to not go after his gem.

After a long and tiresome journey, the green knight worried not that he would not reach the tower and gems but worried what the orange knight would do with unlimited power. So once the green knight made it down to the bottom of the tower, he paused, realizing he could leave the green gem, and took the orange gem instead. Seeing it as a win-win, not having to worry about going mad with power and preventing the orange knight from using the gem for evil.

I knew my brother saw himself in the green knight. Great perseverance, and only wanting to prevent power to keep bad things from happening. I kept it a secret, however, that the last illustration in the book was of the orange knight crying and splashing around the water looking for his gem, calling out to the Oracle that he had been cheated and he had only done as she asked.

His obsession and sadness broke my heart. I wondered how long he stayed in the tower crying. How long something like that could haunt an evil man. The illustration showed a sadness and a want that was like nothing else. At what point do you leave? I had to remind myself that he was evil. I knew though, that my heart went out to the orange knight.

The next few months were when I really realized I was losing Kurt. He now had a caretaker who watched over all of us kids like hawks. Kurt was hardly allowed to leave the house, let alone the grounds, and was only allowed to touch soft objects. It had an alarming effect. I felt like I was made of spikes and needles, the world seemed so much bigger, scarier, and pointier. I wore shoes in the house to prevent myself from slipping and causing damage to Kurt. Rima hardly went near Kurt after getting yelled at for bringing a porcelain doll and a particularly pointy hairbrush to the dining table. Kurt wasn't allowed to eat with knives and all his forks were shaved down to pathetically short and smooth prongs.

My father was clear about all these rules but treated them as mere formality, telling Kurt this was only logical for someone of Kurt's worth. He shouldn't look at the oddity of all this, but the meaning.

It didn't take long for my responsible, rule-following, golden child older brother to snap.

At dinner one night, Kurt was trying to spool up his pasta, but the pathetic fork continued to drop his food. It was mostly silent, but my brother's tension and anger had been growing for weeks, and the minutes at the dinner table slogged on with agony.

At the time I thought my father was unaware of my brother's anger, seeing as it had never been present before. Looking back, I think my father might have been testing Kurt, seeing how he reacted under pressure. My father just miscalculated what Kurt was willing to do.

"Father, may I use another fork?" His voice was controlled, but still had an anger unheard of for Kurt.

"No." My dad thumbed another page of his book.

Rima's eyes were big and worried, flashing back and forth between them, looking like she was watching a tennis match with an invisible ball.

Kurt unsuccessfully tried again. "Father—" he started.

"I gave you my answer, Kurt." My father kept his eyes only on the book. "A poor artist blames his tools. The fork is harder to use, but it is still a fork. So, make the fork work."

My brother's motions were swift; the one guard and my dad didn't stop him in time. He grabbed Rima's fork and stabbed his hand.

The prongs had gone straight through to the other side. The

image that bothered me was that the silver tips seemed clean of blood. How, after going through a whole hand, could they have come out the other side clean?

Kurt let it stay in his hand for a moment before cleanly removing it and letting it drop onto the table. The four small holes in his hand gushed blood at an alarming speed, staining the white tablecloth with a swift puddle. The fork now not only covered, but the center of the bloody puddle.

Then Kurt rested his blond head back and moved his brilliant blue eyes to an exhausted half-open glaze and smiled with pure relief. Like he had scratched an itch or tongued a cut on the roof of his mouth. It was clearly something he had wanted to do for weeks.

Rima sobbed into her pasta.

I didn't know all the words my father used until I was older, but Kurt knew them. Kurt knew exactly what he had done and got exactly what he had wanted, staying calm through it all. He had, after all, meant to elicit my dad's reaction. He knew my dad cared about his physical worth, his image far more than he ever would.

When my brother was fourteen, he began following my father's rules more closely, not for our father but because something finally made him care about his own autonomy.

When Chiffon showed up.

Chiffon was our youngest guard at sixteen and he made a point to particularly watch over Kurt when he was in the flowerbeds, which wasn't entirely odd since gardening was pathetically the most dangerous thing Kurt was allowed to do.

One day, I noticed Rima sniggering by her playroom window. "Come look at this," she called over to me.

I peered out the window to see my brother pressed against his guard and tongue deep in his throat.

After that, my brother was both more careful and seemed happier. Although not talked about, it was one of the worst kept secrets in our house that Kurt and Chiffon were that of a couple. By the time he was seventeen and Chiffon was nineteen, they practically mimicked marriage.

But then, my father twisted that knife between him and Kurt.

My brother was set to be married to Princess Aslinn of the utmost northern kingdom. His wife would come within a year and he would officially be made king.

"Missing?" I rubbed my eyes and blinked hard to adjust to the dark room. "What do you mean Kurt's missing?"

Markus took my hand and walked me out of my wing to the downstairs dining room.

Passing by, I saw bloody sheets being taken from Kurt's room. "Do you know if he's—" I began.

"No," Markus said quickly, but he turned back to give me a sympathetic smile.

Once in the dining room, I was taken aback by my father's look. My father's eyes bagged over, and his face was dark from not sleep deprivation but anger.

Rima, however, seemed more curious than scared.

Markus then informed my father, "We checked, Your Honor, and as you keenly suspected, the guard Chiffon is also missing."

My father's jaw was set, and he seemed to almost be chewing his teeth in rage. "After all I have insured for him," he scoffed. He really truly scoffed. "My bastard fakes a death and takes his incapable body to the world. He's a damned broken infant, incapable of any job other than the one he was bred for!" He slammed his fist on the table. We all stood around in silence for a moment.

Then my father exhaled. It seemed that for the first time, I was really seeing his age, his salt and pepper hair, and the lines that carved his face. To my surprise, he seemed to become calmer, and then looked at me.

He was looking at me.

Before he spoke it was so odd, he really was looking me in the eye. I felt actually seen by him, recognition and focus on me in his eyes. Were his eyes always so gray? He seemed to be sizing me up, looking me up and down.

"Markus, have the king robes resized to Ansel's measurements and send a telegram that Princess Aslinn will be set to marry Ansel instead."

They were so formal and almost unfeeling that the words seemed to slowly form in my tired mind. But my father was really saying what I thought he was saying.

I was going to be king.

A feverish sensation came over my body, a stress, and a tension that I had never known.

Maybe I had dreamed of it, thought bitterly of my brother, but had I ever actually wanted it? Was it just a cool job that I had only wanted because I couldn't have it? Because it belonged to the person I admired and loved most.

I was backing away, hardly registering my father's instructions to the guards. Or Rima's almost entertained face, like she was watching something the way she had always wanted it to play out.

But like before, the moment I could back up, the ice was broken. I turned and ran. I was running through the left wing and knew I couldn't run to my suite, so I ran up to the second story and found myself on the balcony. I supposed jumping off a balcony was one way down. The grass wasn't near as soft as I hoped, but my mind's racing also helped me not feel the pain. I continued over the wall and off. Way past all our grounds, it wasn't until I had reached the beach that I stopped. Collapsing onto the sand, tears going down each side of my face and tickling my ears. *I can't really be a king.* In a weird way, I had never considered that Kurt would always have me if he was king, but if I was a king, then I would never have his help.

It was daytime when Rima woke me up. I never asked how she had gotten away too, but she was there, nonetheless. All of twelve years old but she was similar to Kurt in her young maturity. She sat next to me, ruining her peach nightgown in the wet sand.

"I can't do this, Rima." I thought I was done crying, but another tear left my eye as I looked up at her.

Her eyes were clear of tears but did showcase a worry. She seemed tense, trying to think of better words than what she was going to say. "I know, Ansel."

"I wish he was here." I wanted to think of something better than that, because it really sounded dumb, but just having him back would fit it.

Rima laid down next to me and didn't talk for a moment. We both just sat and breathed. "I think," she said, now picking her words carefully, "Kurt maybe would have been king; he seemed the type who could do the job for forever." She breathed in slowly. "But I think enough things stacked against him to feel trapped."

She was right. Dad had always underestimated the lengths Kurt was willing to go to. I stopped. "I think I underestimated the lengths Kurt was willing to go to."

Rima sighed. "Yeah."

Another tear left my eye as I seemed to be looking down the barrel of a gun, my life had always been laid out in front of me. But now it really was, I felt already carved into stone, remembered by history simply because of a royal title. But would I ever enjoy myself?

"You'll be here for me, right?" I was being a wimp, childishly asking for my younger sister to save me from a nightmare.

She nodded. Now fully to me as I had felt to Kurt.

Baby Teeth

"Okay," Imogen began, "so, what's this theory you have?"

"I think adults forget what it's like to be kids. Not all together, they remember being kids and arguably are in search of quite a bit of what is lost in childhood." Clarissa was the oddest teacher Imogen had worked for yet, even so, the batshit words that came out of this woman's mouth, the sort that compelled Imogen to listen. Even now, having drinks at Clarissa's house.

Clarissa drained her margarita and looked at Imogen with half-lidded eyes. "Like for someone to notice and point out when they've done something well or good. Boy does that dwindle with age, but if I could give any main point as to how grown-ups forget what it's like to be a kid, it's baby teeth." Clarissa let her point drop, then got up from her dining room table and moved over to her blender.

"Baby teeth?" Imogen's eyebrows contracted. "What do you mean? Adults lose teeth." Imogen typically could see where Clarissa's stories were going, but this? Teeth?

"Adults don't lose teeth, not like kids, not like baby teeth. It fascinates me. Really fascinates me." Clarissa had the drunken flush and nod, but forever grounded by her two-inch manicured nails around her glass.

"It would seem like the sort of thing we would prevent for our children at all costs if we could. Few images are as striking as a kid running up smiling with a wide bleeding gap and holding up a tooth to you. If it wasn't a natural thing, I can only imagine the sort of horrified look that could come over someone if their toddler lost a tooth." Clarissa let out a laugh.

"What, you think losing teeth breaks some sort of parental protectiveness?" Imogen crossed her legs and watched her mentor blend away at her what was to be her third lime green margarita.

"Ohhh yeah." Clarissa nodded exaggeratedly. "Losing teeth plagues children constantly, all the time for years they are ripping and bleeding from the gums. Some are precious about it, cry at the pain and beg for something to 'fix' the problem." Clarissa stopped pouring the ghostbuster-green ice mixture long enough to do the air quotes herself. "Whether they want a string tied around the problem, ask for someone else to do it for them, or to wait it out, for the problem tooth to fall out on its own. Some kids are just the type to hate ripping out their own teeth. I know I was." She took a long sip of her fresh drink.

"Of course, that flipside," Clarissa continued, wiped her chin with her finger and held out the same finger to let Imogen know to pause her thought. "I wouldn't really say any kid loves ripping out teeth per se. But there are the kids who have more of that gusto. Who dig their fingers in and passionately and personally take on the strength they can muster to force their tooth out."

"But adults are all people who once did that, I know I remember my teeth falling out." Imogen placed a small hand around her own drink, letting the small buzz let her consider Clarissa's idea.

"Let's say your front tooth was loose right now, would you pull it out or wait for it to fall out?" Clarissa pushed her once intricately curled blonde hair over her shoulder. Now, at the end of the night, she had a sort of backlit frizz around her whole head.

Imogen figured a question like this was coming, but

pondered, looking at the condensation on her cup. "Well, I wouldn't want to lose it, of course, maybe I couldn't say." Imogen pushed her own brown hair back but kept her eyes above Clarissa, deep in thought. "Maybe if it hurt, I would pull it, but I would probably do whatever I could to keep it in. It would probably fall out before I could make up my mind." Imogen let out a low chuckle at the idea.

"Yes. Exactly." Clarissa leaned forward; her half-lidded eyes mustered the strength to fully open. "I think kids know that adults have lost this sort of guts – that kids are weirdly prepared for the pain of ripping out teeth over and over again, year after year. I can't imagine being at the office and turning over in the bathroom to a coworker ripping a tooth out. Blood all over the sink, staining their wonderful business clothing. Adults, we can't handle it any more." Clarissa became animated, moving her drink to and fro, miming the blood getting everywhere.

Clarissa leaned forward, her grip strengthened around her glass, and continued, "We just watch the kids do it, and do it with their rightful tears, and, on occasion, their wonderful rich sense of pride. I think deep down, kids understand those embarrassing moments between each other. Like a nod to someone with the same car as you, the kids know toothache. The bloody face. The relief." Clarissa moved her own eyes up, then let her lids fall half down again, having finished her thought.

Imogen pondered this; maybe the most passionately rowdy kids and the sensitive kids were experiencing the first real thing their parents couldn't save them from – their baby teeth.